THE NETWORKED MIND

The Networked Mind

Alexia Winterbourne

CONTENTS

1 – Introduction 1
2 – Chapter 1: Genesis 5
3 – Chapter 2: The Breakthrough . . 21
4 – Chapter 3: Public Unveiling 41
5 – Chapter 4: Early Adoption 61
6 – Chapter 5: Unintended Consequences 81
7 – Chapter 6: The Dark Side 101
8 – Chapter 7: Global Crisis 121
9 – Chapter 8: The Search for Answers 143
10 – Chapter 9: Redemption 165
11 – Chapter 10: New Beginnings . . . 185
12 – Chapter 11: The Network Expands 205
13 – Chapter 12: Hidden Agendas . 227

14	Chapter 13: The Resistance	249
15	Chapter 14: The Final Showdown	271
16	Chapter 15: Legacy	291

Copyright © 2024 by Alexia Winterbourne

All rights reserved. No part of this book may be reproduced in any manner whatsoever without written permission except in the case of brief quotations embodied in critical articles and reviews.

First Printing, 2024

1

INTRODUCTION

In the not-so-distant future, the world stands on the brink of a technological revolution. The Global Consciousness Network (GCN), a groundbreaking innovation, promises to connect human minds in ways previously unimaginable. At the heart of this revolution is Dr. Emily Carter, a brilliant neuroscientist driven by a vision of a more connected and empathetic world.

Emily's journey began with a simple yet profound question: What if we could truly understand each other? What if the barriers of language, culture, and individual experience could be transcended by a shared consciousness? Her relentless pursuit of this dream led to the creation of the GCN, a network capable of linking human thoughts and emotions, fostering unprecedented levels of communication and collaboration.

As the GCN is unveiled to the world, it sparks a wave of excitement and controversy. Early adopters experience the thrill of shared experiences, while skeptics raise concerns about privacy, individuality, and the potential for misuse. Emily finds herself at the center of a global debate, navigating the complex landscape of ethical dilemmas, political pressures, and personal sacrifices.

But as the GCN expands, unforeseen consequences begin to emerge. Reports of mental overload, loss of identity, and security breaches threaten to undermine the very foundation of Emily's creation. A hacker group exploits the network's vulnerabilities, plunging the world into chaos and fear. Emily, along with her estranged brother Alex, must confront these challenges head-on, seeking to restore balance and security to the GCN.

"The Networked Mind" is a thrilling exploration of the possibilities and perils of a connected world. It delves into the profound questions of what it means to be human in an age where minds can merge, and individuality can be both a strength and a vulnerability. Through Emily's journey, we witness the triumphs and tribulations of innovation, the complexities of ethical responsibility, and the enduring power of human connection.

As you embark on this journey, prepare to question the boundaries of consciousness, the nature of identity, and the future of our interconnected world. Welcome to "The Networked Mind."

2

CHAPTER 1: GENESIS

The Vision

Dr. Emily Carter stood in the center of her futuristic laboratory, surrounded by a symphony of blinking lights and humming machines. The air was thick with the scent of antiseptic and the faint whir of cooling fans. She gazed at the holographic display in front of her, where a complex neural network pulsed with simulated activity. This was the culmination of years of relentless research and sleepless nights—a dream she had nurtured since childhood.

"Mark, can you believe it?" Emily's voice was filled with a mix of awe and excitement as she turned to her assistant, Dr. Mark Thompson. He was a tall, bespectacled man with a calm demeanor that often balanced Emily's fiery passion.

Mark adjusted his glasses and smiled. "It's incredible, Emily. We've come so far. But you know, this is just the beginning."

Emily nodded, her eyes sparkling with determination. "I know. But think about what this means. A global consciousness network—people truly understanding each other, sharing thoughts and emotions. It could change everything."

Mark's smile faded slightly as he considered the implications. "It could. But we have to be careful. There are so many variables, so many things that could go wrong."

Emily sighed, her gaze drifting back to the holographic display. "I understand the risks, Mark. But the potential benefits are too great to ignore. Imagine a world where misunderstandings are a thing of the past, where empathy and collaboration are the norm."

Mark placed a reassuring hand on her shoulder. "I believe in your vision, Emily. But we need to proceed with caution. The ethical implications alone are staggering."

Emily turned to face him, her expression resolute. "That's why we need to be transparent and involve as many perspectives as possible. We can't do this alone."

Mark nodded, appreciating her commitment to ethical responsibility. "Agreed. So, what's next?"

Emily's eyes lit up with renewed energy. "Next, we prepare for the first live test. I want to see how our volunteers respond to the GCN. If we can prove that this works, it will be a game-changer."

Mark chuckled softly. "You always did aim high, Emily. Let's make sure we're ready for anything."

As they continued to discuss the technical details and potential challenges, Emily couldn't help but feel a surge of hope. This was her chance to make a real difference, to create a world where people could connect on a deeper level. She knew the road ahead would be fraught with obstacles, but she was ready to face them head-on.

In that moment, surrounded by the hum of technology and the promise of a brighter future, Emily Carter felt more alive than ever. The vision she had carried for so long was finally within reach, and she was determined to see it through, no matter the cost.

The Experiment

The laboratory was a hive of activity as Dr. Emily Carter and her team prepared for the first live test of the Global Consciousness Network. The air buzzed with anticipation and the faint hum of high-tech equipment. Emily moved through the room with purpose, her mind racing with a mix of excitement and anxiety.

"Alright, everyone, let's make sure everything is in place," Emily called out, her voice steady despite the butterflies in her stomach. She glanced at the array of monitors displaying real-time data from the neural interfaces. Each volunteer was seated in a comfortable chair, electrodes carefully placed on their temples, ready to connect their minds to the network.

Dr. Mark Thompson stood by her side, clipboard in hand. "All systems are green, Emily. We're ready when you are."

Emily took a deep breath and approached the group of volunteers. They were a diverse mix of individuals—scientists, students, and everyday people—each chosen for their willingness to explore the unknown. She could see the excitement and nervousness in their eyes, mirroring her own feelings.

"Thank you all for being here," Emily began, her voice warm and reassuring. "Today, we're taking a monumental step forward. The Global Consciousness Network has the potential to revolutionize how we connect and understand each other. Your participation is crucial, and I want you to know how much it means to us."

One of the volunteers, a young woman named Sarah, raised her hand. "What exactly should we expect to feel during the test?"

Emily smiled. "Great question, Sarah. You might experience shared thoughts, emotions, and even memories with the other participants. It's important to stay calm and open-minded. If at any point you feel uncomfortable, just let us know, and we'll disconnect you immediately."

With a nod from Sarah and the other volunteers, Emily turned to Mark. "Let's begin."

Mark initiated the sequence, and the room filled with a soft, rhythmic hum as the neural interfaces activated. Emily watched the monitors closely, her heart pounding. The data streams showed the volunteers' brainwaves syncing, their neural patterns beginning to align.

"How are you all feeling?" Emily asked, her eyes scanning the room.

A middle-aged man named David spoke up first. "It's... strange, but not unpleasant. I can sense thoughts that aren't mine, like echoes in my mind."

Sarah nodded in agreement. "I feel a wave of emotions, like I'm tapping into a collective consciousness. It's overwhelming but fascinating."

As the experiment progressed, the volunteers' experiences grew more intense. Some laughed, sharing joyful memories, while others shed tears, touched by the profound connections they were forming. Emily felt a surge of pride and relief. The GCN was working.

Suddenly, one of the monitors flashed red. Emily's heart skipped a beat. "Mark, what's happening?"

Mark quickly analyzed the data. "One of the volunteers is experiencing a spike in neural activity. It looks like an emotional overload."

Emily rushed to the volunteer, a young man named Jason, who was gripping the arms of his chair, his face contorted in distress. "Jason, can you hear me? We're going to disconnect you now."

With swift precision, Mark deactivated Jason's neural interface. The young man gasped, his body relaxing as the connection was severed. "I'm okay," he panted. "It was just too much, too fast."

Emily placed a comforting hand on his shoulder. "Thank you for your bravery, Jason. We'll make adjustments to ensure this doesn't happen again."

As the experiment concluded, Emily addressed the group once more. "You've all been incredible. This is just the beginning, and your feedback will help us improve the GCN. Together, we're making history."

The volunteers smiled, their initial apprehension replaced by a sense of accomplishment. Emily felt a wave of gratitude wash over her. Despite the challenges, they were on the right path. The vision of a connected world was becoming a reality, one step at a time.

Personal Stakes

The sun had long set by the time Dr. Emily Carter returned home, her mind still buzzing with the day's events. She dropped her bag by the door and sank into the plush sofa, the weight of exhaustion settling over her. The first live test of the Global Consciousness Network had been a success, but the emotional overload experienced by one of the volunteers lingered in her thoughts.

Emily reached for her phone, hesitating for a moment before dialing a familiar number. The line rang twice before a voice answered.

"Emily? It's been a while," came the voice of her estranged brother, Alex. There was a hint of surprise and wariness in his tone.

"Hi, Alex," Emily replied, trying to keep her voice steady. "I wanted to share some news with you. We had our first live test of the GCN today. It was... incredible."

There was a pause on the other end. "The Global Consciousness Network? So, you actually went through with it."

"Yes, we did," Emily said, a note of pride creeping into her voice. "The volunteers experienced shared thoughts and emotions. It was like nothing I've ever seen before."

Alex's skepticism was palpable even through the phone. "And what about the risks? The ethical concerns? Have you thought about what could go wrong?"

Emily sighed, rubbing her temples. "Of course, we have. We're taking every precaution, but this is groundbreaking work, Alex. It has the potential to change the world for the better."

"Or for the worse," Alex countered. "You know how I feel about this, Emily. Connecting minds sounds great in theory, but what about privacy? Individuality? What happens when people start losing themselves in this network?"

Emily's frustration bubbled to the surface. "We're aware of the risks, and we're addressing them. But we can't let fear hold us back from progress. This could bring people closer together, help us understand each other in ways we never thought possible."

Alex's voice softened slightly. "I know you're passionate about this, Em. But sometimes, the road to hell is paved with good intentions. Just... be careful, okay?"

Emily felt a pang of sadness. Despite their differences, she missed her brother. "I will, Alex. I promise. I just wish you could see the potential like I do."

There was a long silence before Alex spoke again. "Maybe one day. Take care of yourself, Emily."

"You too, Alex," she replied, her voice barely above a whisper.

As the call ended, Emily stared at her phone, a mix of emotions swirling within her. She knew Alex's concerns were valid, but she couldn't shake the feeling that the GCN was a step in the right direction. The vision she had carried for so long was finally taking shape, and she was determined to see it through.

Emily leaned back on the sofa, closing her eyes. The day's events replayed in her mind—the excitement of the experiment, the volunteers' reactions, the unexpected challenges. She knew the road ahead would be difficult, but she was ready to face whatever came her way.

In the quiet of her home, Emily resolved to push forward, driven by the hope that one day, the world would understand the true potential of the Global Consciousness Network. And perhaps, in time, even Alex would come to see the possibilities it held.

Ethical Dilemmas

The conference room at the research facility was filled with a palpable tension as Dr. Emily Carter prepared to present the results of the initial tests of the Global Consciousness Network to a panel of ethics advisors. The room was stark and modern, with a long glass table and sleek chairs. The advisors, a diverse group of experts in neuroscience, ethics, and law, sat in a semicircle, their expressions a mix of curiosity and skepticism.

Emily took a deep breath and began her presentation, her voice steady and confident. "Thank you all for being here today. As you know, the Global Consciousness Network aims to connect human minds, allowing for unprecedented levels of empathy and understanding. Our initial tests have shown promising results, with volunteers experiencing shared thoughts and emotions."

She clicked a button on her remote, and a series of graphs and images appeared on the large screen behind her. "These are the brainwave patterns of our volunteers before and during the connection. As you can see, there's a significant alignment, indicating successful synchronization."

Dr. Helen Ramirez, a renowned ethicist, leaned forward, her brow furrowed. "Dr. Carter, while the data is impressive, there are serious ethical concerns that need to be addressed. What measures are you taking to ensure the privacy and autonomy of the individuals connected to the GCN?"

Emily nodded, anticipating the question. "We've implemented strict protocols to protect user privacy. Each connection is encrypted, and participants have full control over their level of engagement. They can disconnect at any time. Additionally, we're working on safeguards to prevent unauthorized access and misuse."

Dr. Michael Lee, a legal expert, interjected. "But what about the potential for coercion or manipulation? If someone gains control over the network, they could influence the thoughts and actions of others. How do you plan to mitigate that risk?"

Emily's gaze shifted to Mark, who gave her a reassuring nod. "We're aware of the potential for abuse, Dr. Lee. That's why we're collaborating with cybersecurity experts to develop robust defenses against hacking and unauthorized control. We're also establishing an independent oversight committee to monitor the network and ensure ethical standards are upheld."

Dr. Ramirez wasn't convinced. "Even with these measures, the psychological impact on individuals could be profound. Shared thoughts and emotions might lead to a loss of personal identity. Have you considered the long-term effects on mental health?"

Emily took a deep breath, her mind racing. "Yes, we have. We're conducting ongoing psychological assessments of our volunteers to monitor their well-being. So far, the feedback has been overwhelmingly positive, but we recognize the need for continuous evaluation and support."

The room fell silent as the advisors absorbed her words. Emily could feel the weight of their scrutiny, the enormity of the responsibility she carried. She knew that convincing them was crucial for the future of the GCN.

Dr. Lee spoke again, his tone more measured. "Dr. Carter, your dedication to this project is clear, and the potential benefits are undeniable. However, the ethical implications are equally significant. We need to ensure that this technology is developed and deployed responsibly."

Emily nodded, her resolve unwavering. "I understand, Dr. Lee. That's why we're committed to transparency and collaboration. We want to work with you to address these concerns and create a framework that prioritizes ethical responsibility."

Dr. Ramirez leaned back in her chair, her expression thoughtful. "Very well, Dr. Carter. We'll need to see detailed plans and ongoing reports, but for now, you have our cautious support. Proceed with care."

Relief washed over Emily as she thanked the panel and concluded the meeting. As she and Mark left the conference room, she felt a renewed sense of purpose. The path ahead was fraught with challenges, but with the support of the ethics advisors, she was more determined than ever to ensure that the Global Consciousness Network would be a force for good.

In the quiet hallway, Mark turned to her with a smile. "You did great, Emily. We're one step closer."

Emily smiled back, her heart swelling with hope. "Thanks, Mark. Now, let's get back to work. We've got a lot to do."

The Decision

The laboratory was eerily quiet, the usual hum of activity replaced by the soft glow of monitors and the occasional beep of equipment. It was late, and most of the team had gone home, leaving Dr. Emily Carter and Dr. Mark Thompson to work in solitude. The day's events weighed heavily on Emily's mind as she reviewed the data from the initial test of the Global Consciousness Network.

"Mark, can you pull up the feedback from the volunteers?" Emily asked, her eyes fixed on the screen in front of her.

Mark nodded and tapped a few keys on his tablet. "Here it is. Overall, the responses are positive, but there are a few concerns about the intensity of the shared experiences."

Emily scanned the feedback, her brow furrowing. "We need to find a way to moderate the intensity. The emotional overload Jason experienced can't happen again."

Mark leaned back in his chair, rubbing his temples. "It's a delicate balance. We want the connections to be meaningful, but we also need to ensure they're safe."

Emily sighed, her mind racing with possibilities. "We could implement a tiered system, allowing users to gradually increase their level of connection. That might help them acclimate to the experience."

Mark nodded thoughtfully. "That could work. We should also consider adding more safeguards to prevent unauthorized access. The ethics panel's concerns were valid, and we need to address them."

Emily's thoughts drifted to the meeting with the ethics advisors. Their support was crucial, but it came with a heavy burden of responsibility. She knew they were right to be cautious, and she was determined to prove that the GCN could be both revolutionary and ethical.

"Mark, I want to move forward with the public unveiling," Emily said, her voice resolute. "But we need to make sure we're fully prepared. Let's refine the system and address the feedback. We can't afford any mistakes."

Mark gave her a reassuring smile. "We'll get it done, Emily. This project is too important to rush, but it's also too important to abandon. We'll find the right balance."

Emily felt a surge of gratitude for Mark's unwavering support. "Thank you, Mark. I couldn't do this without you."

As they continued to work late into the night, Emily's determination only grew stronger. She knew the road ahead would be challenging, but she was ready to face whatever obstacles came their way. The vision of a connected world, where empathy and understanding transcended barriers, was worth fighting for.

In the quiet of the laboratory, surrounded by the tools of their groundbreaking work, Emily and Mark forged ahead, driven by a shared belief in the potential of the Global Consciousness Network. They knew that the decisions they made now would shape the future, and they were committed to ensuring that future was one of hope and possibility.

As the first light of dawn began to filter through the windows, Emily felt a renewed sense of purpose. The journey was just beginning, and she was ready to lead the way. With Mark by her side and the support of her team, she knew they could overcome any challenge.

Together, they would make the vision of the Networked Mind a reality.

3
CHAPTER 2: THE BREAKTHROUGH

Preparations

The laboratory was bathed in the soft glow of early morning light, casting long shadows across the sleek, modern equipment. Dr. Emily Carter stood at the center of the room, her eyes scanning the array of monitors and devices that surrounded her. Today was the day they would test the full capabilities of the Global Consciousness Network, and the air was thick with anticipation.

"Alright, team, let's go over the procedures one more time," Emily called out, her voice steady and authoritative. Her research team, a group of dedicated scientists and engineers, gathered around her, their faces a mix of excitement and nervous energy.

Dr. Mark Thompson, Emily's trusted assistant, stepped forward with a clipboard in hand. "We've double-checked all the connections and calibrated the neural interfaces. The volunteers are scheduled to arrive in an hour. We'll start with a brief orientation before we begin the test."

Emily nodded, her mind racing with a thousand thoughts. "Good. Remember, safety is our top priority. If anyone experiences discomfort or distress, we need to be ready to intervene immediately."

The team members nodded in agreement, their expressions serious. Emily could see the determination in their eyes, a reflection of her own resolve. They had worked tirelessly to reach this point, and now it was time to see if their efforts would pay off.

As the team dispersed to finalize the preparations, Emily moved to her workstation, where a series of holographic displays showed real-time data from the neural interfaces. She tapped a few keys, bringing up the latest diagnostics. Everything seemed to be in order, but she couldn't shake the feeling of unease that lingered at the back of her mind.

"Emily, we've got a problem," Mark's voice broke through her thoughts. She turned to see him frowning at one of the monitors. "The synchronization module is showing some irregularities. It might cause a delay."

Emily's heart sank. They couldn't afford any setbacks, not today. "Let's take a look," she said, moving to his side. Together, they examined the data, their minds working in tandem to identify the issue.

After a few tense minutes, Emily spotted the problem. "It's a calibration error. We need to adjust the frequency modulation. Mark, can you handle the software update while I recalibrate the hardware?"

Mark nodded, already tapping away at his tablet. "On it."

Emily moved swiftly, her hands deftly adjusting the delicate components of the synchronization module. She could feel the pressure mounting, but she forced herself to stay focused. This was too important to rush.

As she worked, she couldn't help but think about the potential impact of the GCN. If successful, it could revolutionize the way people connected and communicated. But the risks were equally significant. The ethical dilemmas and potential for misuse weighed heavily on her mind.

"Emily, I've updated the software. How's the hardware looking?" Mark's voice brought her back to the present.

"Just about done," she replied, making a final adjustment. "There. That should do it."

They ran a quick diagnostic, and this time, the synchronization module showed a stable reading. Emily let out a sigh of relief. "Great job, Mark. Let's get everything else ready."

As the team continued their preparations, Emily took a moment to reflect. They were on the brink of something extraordinary, but the path ahead was fraught with challenges. She knew they had to proceed with caution, balancing their ambition with a deep sense of responsibility.

With the final preparations complete, Emily gathered the team once more. "This is it, everyone. Today, we take a major step forward. Let's make sure we're ready for anything."

The team responded with a collective nod, their determination palpable. Emily felt a surge of pride and gratitude. They were in this together, and she knew they would give it their all.

As the first volunteers began to arrive, Emily took a deep breath, steeling herself for the task ahead. The future of the Global Consciousness Network was in their hands, and she was ready to lead the way.

The Test Begins

The laboratory buzzed with a heightened sense of anticipation as the volunteers settled into their designated seats. Each chair was equipped with a sleek neural interface, designed to connect their minds to the Global Consciousness Network. Dr. Emily Carter moved among them, offering reassuring smiles and words of encouragement.

"Remember, if at any point you feel uncomfortable, just let us know," Emily said, her voice calm and steady. She could see the mixture of excitement and nervousness in their eyes, mirroring her own emotions.

Dr. Mark Thompson stood by the main console, his fingers flying over the controls. "All systems are green, Emily. We're ready to initiate the connection."

Emily took a deep breath and nodded. "Let's begin."

Mark activated the sequence, and the room filled with a soft, rhythmic hum as the neural interfaces powered up. The volunteers closed their eyes, their expressions a mix of concentration and curiosity. Emily watched the monitors closely, her heart pounding in her chest. The data streams showed the volunteers' brainwaves beginning to sync, their neural patterns aligning with the network.

"How are you all feeling?" Emily asked, her eyes scanning the room.

A young woman named Sarah opened her eyes and smiled. "It's like... I can sense everyone else. It's strange but amazing."

David, a middle-aged man with a thoughtful expression, nodded in agreement. "I feel a connection, like we're all part of something bigger."

Emily's heart swelled with pride. The initial signs were promising, but she knew they had to remain vigilant. "Great. Just relax and let the connection deepen."

As the minutes passed, the volunteers began to experience more profound connections. They shared thoughts, emotions, and even fragments of memories. Laughter and tears filled the room as they navigated the new and unfamiliar sensations.

Suddenly, one of the monitors flashed red. Emily's pulse quickened. "Mark, what's happening?"

Mark quickly analyzed the data. "It's Jason. His neural activity is spiking. He might be experiencing discomfort."

Emily rushed to Jason's side. He was gripping the arms of his chair, his face contorted in distress. "Jason, can you hear me? We're going to adjust the settings."

She signaled to Mark, who made rapid adjustments to the interface. The red alert on the monitor subsided, and Jason's expression relaxed. He took a deep breath and nodded. "I'm okay now. It was just... overwhelming for a moment."

Emily placed a comforting hand on his shoulder. "Thank you for letting us know. We'll continue to monitor and make sure everyone is comfortable."

The test resumed, and the volunteers continued to explore the depths of their shared consciousness. Emily and Mark monitored the data closely, ready to intervene at the first sign of trouble. The initial scare had heightened their awareness, but it also reinforced the importance of their work.

As the test progressed, the volunteers began to share more profound insights. Sarah spoke of a childhood memory, vividly reliving the emotions and sensations. David shared a moment of deep personal loss, and the group collectively felt his sorrow and offered silent support.

Emily watched in awe as the connections deepened. The GCN was working, creating a tapestry of shared human experience. It was a glimpse into a future where empathy and understanding could transcend individual boundaries.

"Emily, look at this," Mark said, pointing to a monitor. "The synchronization is holding steady. The connections are stable."

Emily felt a surge of relief. "That's incredible, Mark. We're seeing something truly extraordinary here."

The test continued for another hour, with the volunteers sharing and exploring their interconnected minds. When it finally came time to disconnect, there was a palpable sense of reluctance. The volunteers had experienced something unique and profound, and they were reluctant to let it go.

"Thank you all for your participation," Emily said, her voice filled with gratitude. "Your feedback will be invaluable as we move forward."

As the volunteers left the laboratory, Emily and Mark began the process of analyzing the data. The initial results were promising, but there was still much work to be done. They needed to refine the system, address the issues that had arisen, and prepare for the next phase.

In the quiet of the laboratory, Emily felt a renewed sense of purpose. The breakthrough they had achieved today was just the beginning. The Global Consciousness Network had the potential to change the world, and she was determined to see it through.

"Great job today, Mark," Emily said, turning to her colleague. "Let's get to work on the next steps."

Mark smiled, his eyes reflecting the same determination. "Absolutely, Emily. We're just getting started."

Unexpected Insights

The laboratory was filled with a quiet hum as the test continued. Dr. Emily Carter and Dr. Mark Thompson monitored the data closely, their eyes flicking between the screens and the volunteers. The initial tension had eased, replaced by a sense of wonder as the volunteers began to share their experiences.

"Emily, look at this," Mark said, pointing to one of the monitors. "The synchronization is holding steady. The connections are stable."

Emily nodded, her eyes shining with excitement. "This is incredible, Mark. We're seeing something truly extraordinary here."

The volunteers were deep in their shared consciousness, their faces reflecting a range of emotions. Sarah, the young woman who had been so enthusiastic earlier, spoke up, her voice filled with awe. "I can see a memory from when I was a child, playing in the park with my parents. It's so vivid, like I'm there again."

David, the middle-aged man, nodded. "I can feel that memory too, Sarah. It's beautiful. I can sense the joy and love you felt."

Emily watched as the volunteers continued to share their thoughts and emotions. The GCN was creating a tapestry of interconnected human experience, each thread adding to the richness of the whole. It was a glimpse into a future where empathy and understanding could transcend individual boundaries.

Suddenly, one of the volunteers, a young man named Jason, spoke up. His voice was shaky, and his eyes were filled with tears. "I'm seeing something... something painful. It's a memory of losing my father. The grief is overwhelming."

The room fell silent as the other volunteers absorbed Jason's emotions. Emily felt a pang of empathy, her heart aching for him. She knew this was a critical moment, a test of the GCN's ability to handle intense emotions.

"Jason, thank you for sharing that," Emily said gently. "It's important that we understand all aspects of this experience, even the difficult ones. How are you feeling now?"

Jason took a deep breath, his expression softening. "It's hard, but... it's also comforting to know that others can understand my pain. It feels less isolating."

Sarah reached out and placed a hand on Jason's arm. "We're here for you, Jason. You're not alone."

Emily watched the interaction, her heart swelling with pride. This was the true power of the GCN—bringing people together in a way that fostered deep empathy and connection. But it also highlighted the need for careful management and support.

"Let's take a moment to process this," Emily said, addressing the group. "If anyone needs a break, please let us know."

The volunteers nodded, their expressions thoughtful. Emily could see that the experience had affected them deeply, but it had also brought them closer together. It was a powerful reminder of the potential and the responsibility that came with the GCN.

As the volunteers continued to share their insights, Emily and Mark monitored the data, noting the patterns and anomalies. They discussed the implications of their findings, the potential for further development, and the need for additional safeguards.

"Emily, the data is showing some unexpected anomalies," Mark said, his brow furrowed. "We need to investigate these further to ensure the long-term stability of the GCN."

Emily nodded, her mind racing with possibilities. "Agreed. We need to address these issues before we move forward. But overall, this has been a remarkable breakthrough."

As the test concluded, Emily addressed the volunteers once more. "Thank you all for your participation. Your feedback is invaluable, and it will help us improve the GCN. Together, we're making history."

The volunteers smiled, their initial apprehension replaced by a sense of accomplishment. Emily felt a wave of gratitude wash over her. Despite the challenges, they were on the right path. The vision of a connected world was becoming a reality, one step at a time.

In the quiet of the laboratory, Emily and Mark began the process of analyzing the data. The initial results were promising, but there was still much work to be done. They needed to refine the system, address the issues that had arisen, and prepare for the next phase.

"Great job today, Mark," Emily said, turning to her colleague. "Let's get to work on the next steps."

Mark smiled, his eyes reflecting the same determination. "Absolutely, Emily. We're just getting started."

Data Analysis

The laboratory was quiet, the hum of the equipment providing a soothing backdrop as Dr. Emily Carter and Dr. Mark Thompson sat at their workstations, surrounded by a sea of data. The initial test of the Global Consciousness Network had concluded, and now it was time to analyze the results. The room was dimly lit, the glow from the monitors casting a soft light on their focused faces.

"Alright, let's dive into the data," Emily said, her fingers flying over the keyboard. She brought up the brainwave patterns from the volunteers, each one a complex tapestry of neural activity. "We need to understand exactly what happened during the test."

Mark nodded, his eyes scanning the screens. "The synchronization was impressive, but we did see some anomalies. Let's start with the overall patterns and then drill down into the specifics."

They worked in silence for a while, the only sounds the clicking of keys and the occasional beep from the machines. Emily felt a mix of excitement and apprehension. The test had been a success, but there were still many questions to answer.

"Look at this," Mark said, pointing to a series of graphs. "These spikes in neural activity correspond to the moments when the volunteers shared particularly intense emotions. It's fascinating, but also a bit concerning."

Emily leaned in, studying the data. "We need to find a way to moderate these spikes. If the emotional intensity is too high, it could lead to overload, like what happened with Jason."

Mark nodded in agreement. "We could implement a feedback loop that adjusts the intensity in real-time, based on the participants' neural responses. It would help maintain a stable connection without overwhelming them."

Emily's mind raced with possibilities. "That's a great idea. We should also consider adding more layers of encryption to protect the data. The ethics panel was right to be concerned about privacy and security."

They continued to analyze the data, discussing the implications of their findings and brainstorming solutions. Emily felt a deep sense of responsibility. The GCN had the potential to change the world, but it also came with significant risks. They had to get it right.

"Emily, take a look at this," Mark said, his voice tinged with excitement. "These patterns here—when the volunteers shared positive memories, their brainwaves showed a remarkable level of coherence. It's like their minds were truly in sync."

Emily's eyes widened as she examined the data. "This is incredible, Mark. It shows that the GCN can foster deep connections and shared understanding. But we need to ensure that these connections are safe and sustainable."

They worked late into the evening, their focus unwavering. The data revealed both the promise and the challenges of the GCN. There were moments of profound connection, but also instances of emotional overload and unexpected anomalies. Emily knew they had to address these issues before moving forward.

As the hours passed, Emily felt a growing sense of determination. They were on the brink of something extraordinary, but they had to proceed with caution. The ethical implications were significant, and they needed to ensure that the GCN was developed responsibly.

"Mark, let's compile a report of our findings and recommendations," Emily said, her voice resolute. "We need to present this to the ethics panel and get their input before we move forward."

Mark nodded, his expression serious. "Agreed. We have a lot of work to do, but I believe in this project. We're making history, Emily."

Emily smiled, feeling a surge of pride and gratitude. "Thank you, Mark. I couldn't do this without you."

As they continued to work, Emily felt a renewed sense of purpose. The journey was far from over, but they were making progress. The Global Consciousness Network had the potential to transform the world, and she was determined to see it through.

In the quiet of the laboratory, surrounded by the tools of their groundbreaking work, Emily and Mark forged ahead, driven by a shared belief in the power of human connection. They knew that the decisions they made now would shape the future, and they were committed to ensuring that future was one of hope and possibility.

"Let's get this right," Emily said, her voice filled with determination. "For everyone."

Mark nodded, his eyes reflecting the same resolve. "For everyone."

Moving Forward

The laboratory was cloaked in the stillness of late night, the only sounds the soft hum of equipment and the occasional click of a keyboard. Dr. Emily Carter sat in her office, the glow from her computer screen casting a gentle light on her thoughtful face. She leaned back in her chair, reflecting on the day's events and the significance of their breakthrough.

The initial test of the Global Consciousness Network had been a success, but it had also revealed the complexities and challenges they faced. Emily knew they had to proceed with caution, balancing their ambition with a deep sense of responsibility.

A knock on the door broke her reverie. "Come in," she called, her voice steady.

Dr. Mark Thompson entered, carrying a stack of reports. "I thought you might want to see the preliminary analysis," he said, placing the papers on her desk. "We've made some incredible progress, but there are definitely areas we need to address."

Emily nodded, her eyes scanning the reports. "Thank you, Mark. The feedback from the volunteers has been invaluable. We need to refine the system and address the anomalies we observed."

Mark took a seat across from her, his expression serious. "The emotional overload that Jason experienced was a wake-up call. We need to implement safeguards to prevent that from happening again. And the ethical concerns raised by the panel are valid. We have to ensure the GCN is secure and respects individual privacy."

Emily sighed, her mind racing with possibilities. "I agree. We need to develop a tiered system that allows users to gradually increase their level of connection. It will help them acclimate to the experience without being overwhelmed."

Mark nodded thoughtfully. "And we should enhance our encryption protocols to protect the data. The last thing we need is for the GCN to be compromised."

Emily felt a surge of gratitude for Mark's unwavering support. "Thank you, Mark. Your insights are invaluable. We're in this together, and I know we can make the GCN a force for good."

They spent the next few hours discussing the next steps, their conversation punctuated by moments of intense focus and bursts of creative energy. Emily felt a renewed sense of purpose as they brainstormed solutions and mapped out their plan.

"Emily, I think we should also consider forming an independent oversight committee," Mark suggested. "It would help address the ethical concerns and provide an additional layer of accountability."

Emily's eyes lit up. "That's a great idea, Mark. It would show our commitment to transparency and ethical responsibility. Let's make it happen."

As the night wore on, Emily and Mark continued to work, their determination unwavering. They knew the road ahead would be challenging, but they were ready to face whatever obstacles came their way. The vision of a connected world, where empathy and understanding transcended barriers, was worth fighting for.

In the quiet of her office, Emily felt a deep sense of resolve. The journey was just beginning, and she was ready to lead the way. With Mark by her side and the support of her team, she knew they could overcome any challenge.

"Great job today, Mark," Emily said, her voice filled with gratitude. "Let's get some rest and start fresh tomorrow. We have a lot of work to do."

Mark smiled, his eyes reflecting the same determination. "Absolutely, Emily. We're just getting started."

As Mark left the office, Emily took a moment to reflect on the day's events. The breakthrough they had achieved was just the beginning. The Global Consciousness Network had the potential to change the world, and she was determined to see it through.

In the stillness of the night, surrounded by the tools of their groundbreaking work, Emily felt a renewed sense of hope. The future was uncertain, but it was also filled with possibility. Together, they would make the vision of the Networked Mind a reality.

4
CHAPTER 3: PUBLIC UNVEILING

The Announcement

The press conference room at the research facility was abuzz with anticipation. Rows of chairs faced a sleek podium, flanked by large screens displaying the logo of the Global Consciousness Network. Media representatives, government officials, and corporate executives filled the room, their conversations a low hum of excitement and curiosity.

Dr. Emily Carter stood behind the podium, her heart pounding with a mix of nerves and exhilaration. She glanced at Dr. Mark Thompson, who gave her an encouraging nod. This was the moment they had been working towards—the public unveiling of the GCN.

Emily took a deep breath and stepped up to the microphone. The room fell silent, all eyes on her. "Good morning, everyone. Thank you for joining us today. My name is Dr. Emily Carter, and I am honored to introduce you to the Global Consciousness Network, a groundbreaking innovation that has the potential to transform the way we connect and understand each other."

She paused, letting her words sink in. The screens behind her came to life, displaying images of the neural interfaces and the volunteers who had participated in the initial tests. "The GCN allows individuals to share thoughts, emotions, and memories, creating a network of interconnected minds. Our initial tests have shown remarkable results, with participants experiencing profound levels of empathy and understanding."

A murmur of interest rippled through the audience. Emily continued, her voice steady and confident. "We believe that the GCN can foster greater collaboration, reduce misunderstandings, and bring people closer together. However, we are also acutely aware of the ethical implications and potential risks. That is why we have implemented strict protocols to ensure privacy, security, and individual autonomy."

She glanced at Mark, who was monitoring the data feeds from the neural interfaces. Everything was running smoothly. Emily turned back to the audience, ready to address the inevitable questions.

A journalist from a major news outlet raised her hand. "Dr. Carter, can you elaborate on the privacy measures you've put in place? How can you guarantee that individuals' thoughts and emotions won't be exploited or misused?"

Emily nodded, prepared for this question. "Each connection within the GCN is encrypted, and participants have full control over their level of engagement. They can disconnect at any time. Additionally, we are working with cybersecurity experts to develop robust defenses against unauthorized access. We are also establishing an independent oversight committee to monitor the network and ensure ethical standards are upheld."

Another hand shot up, this time from a government official. "What about the potential for coercion or manipulation? How do you plan to prevent misuse by those in positions of power?"

Emily's gaze was unwavering. "We recognize the potential for misuse, which is why we are committed to transparency and accountability. The oversight committee will include representatives from various sectors, including ethics, law, and human rights. Our goal is to create a framework that prioritizes ethical responsibility and safeguards against abuse."

The questions continued, ranging from technical details to ethical concerns. Emily answered each one with clarity and conviction, determined to reassure the public about the safety and integrity of the GCN. She could feel the weight of their scrutiny, but she also sensed their growing interest and curiosity.

As the press conference drew to a close, Emily delivered her final remarks. "The Global Consciousness Network represents a new frontier in human connection. We are excited about the possibilities it holds, but we are also committed to ensuring that it is developed responsibly. Together, we can create a future where empathy and understanding transcend boundaries."

The room erupted in applause, and Emily felt a surge of relief and pride. She had faced the skeptics and the doubters, and she had stood her ground. The public unveiling was just the beginning, but it was a crucial step forward.

As the media representatives and officials began to file out, Emily turned to Mark, who was beaming with pride. "You did great, Emily. We're on our way."

Emily smiled, feeling a renewed sense of purpose. "Thank you, Mark. Now, let's get ready for the next phase. There's still a lot of work to do."

In the aftermath of the announcement, Emily felt a mixture of exhaustion and exhilaration. The journey ahead would be challenging, but she was ready to face it head-on. The vision of a connected world was within reach, and she was determined to make it a reality.

Media Frenzy

The announcement of the Global Consciousness Network spread like wildfire. Within hours, news outlets and social media platforms were abuzz with discussions, debates, and speculations about the groundbreaking technology. Dr. Emily Carter and Dr. Mark Thompson found themselves at the center of a media storm, their days filled with interviews and public appearances.

Emily sat in a brightly lit studio, the cameras trained on her as a well-known journalist began the live broadcast. "Good evening, viewers. Tonight, we have a special guest, Dr. Emily Carter, the visionary behind the Global Consciousness Network. Dr. Carter, thank you for joining us."

"Thank you for having me," Emily replied, her voice calm and composed despite the whirlwind of activity around her.

The journalist leaned forward, his expression serious. "Dr. Carter, the GCN has been described as a revolutionary technology that could change the way we connect and communicate. But there are also concerns about privacy and security. How do you address these issues?"

Emily took a deep breath, ready to tackle the tough questions. "The GCN is designed with privacy and security as top priorities. Each connection is encrypted, and participants have full control over their level of engagement. We are also working with cybersecurity experts to develop robust defenses against unauthorized access. Additionally, we are establishing an independent oversight committee to ensure ethical standards are upheld."

The journalist nodded, but his skepticism was evident. "What about the potential for misuse? Could this technology be exploited by those in power to manipulate or control others?"

Emily's gaze was steady. "We recognize the potential risks, which is why we are committed to transparency and accountability. The oversight committee will include representatives from various sectors, including ethics, law, and human rights. Our goal is to create a framework that prioritizes ethical responsibility and safeguards against abuse."

As the interview continued, Emily answered each question with clarity and conviction. She knew that public trust was crucial for the success of the GCN, and she was determined to reassure the audience about its safety and integrity.

Meanwhile, Mark was handling the social media frenzy from the research facility. He monitored the trending topics and responded to questions and comments from the public. The reactions were mixed—some people were excited about the possibilities of the GCN, while others were fearful and skeptical.

"Mark, have you seen this?" one of the team members asked, pointing to a viral tweet. "Someone's claiming that the GCN can be used for mind control. It's spreading like wildfire."

Mark frowned, his fingers flying over the keyboard as he crafted a response. "We need to address this misinformation quickly. Let's put out a statement clarifying how the GCN works and emphasizing the safeguards we've put in place."

The team worked tirelessly to manage the narrative, correcting false information and providing accurate details about the GCN. Emily joined them after her interview, her face flushed with the adrenaline of the day.

"How's it going here?" she asked, glancing at the screens filled with social media feeds and news articles.

Mark looked up, his expression serious. "It's a mixed bag. There's a lot of excitement, but also a lot of fear and misinformation. We're doing our best to keep things under control."

Emily nodded, her mind racing. "We need to be proactive. Let's schedule more interviews and public appearances. We have to keep communicating our message clearly and consistently."

The next few days were a blur of activity. Emily and Mark appeared on talk shows, participated in panel discussions, and gave interviews to major news outlets. They addressed concerns, shared success stories from the initial tests, and emphasized the ethical guidelines they were implementing.

Despite their efforts, the public reaction remained divided. Some people were thrilled by the potential of the GCN, envisioning a future where empathy and understanding transcended boundaries. Others were wary, fearing the loss of privacy and the potential for misuse.

Emily felt the weight of the scrutiny, but she also felt a deep sense of purpose. The journey was challenging, but she was committed to seeing it through. The vision of a connected world was within reach, and she was determined to make it a reality.

As the media frenzy continued, Emily and Mark remained steadfast, navigating the storm with resilience and determination. They knew that the road ahead would be difficult, but they were ready to face whatever challenges came their way.

In the midst of the chaos, Emily found solace in the support of her team and the belief in the transformative power of the GCN. Together, they would forge a path forward, driven by the hope of a better, more connected world.

Government Interest

The government office was a stark contrast to the bustling media frenzy. The meeting room was spacious and formal, with a long mahogany table surrounded by high-backed chairs. Dr. Emily Carter and Dr. Mark Thompson sat at one end, facing a group of government officials and corporate representatives. The atmosphere was tense, filled with a mix of curiosity and skepticism.

"Thank you for coming, Dr. Carter and Dr. Thompson," said Secretary Jameson, a senior government official with a stern demeanor. "We appreciate you taking the time to discuss the Global Consciousness Network with us."

Emily nodded, her expression calm and composed. "Thank you for having us, Secretary Jameson. We're here to provide any information you need and to discuss the potential applications and implications of the GCN."

The screens around the room displayed various data points and visualizations of the GCN's capabilities. Emily and Mark had prepared extensively for this meeting, knowing that government interest could significantly impact the project's future.

"Dr. Carter, the potential applications of the GCN are vast," said Mr. Patel, a representative from a major tech corporation. "From national security to healthcare and education, this technology could revolutionize multiple sectors. Can you elaborate on how you envision these applications?"

Emily leaned forward, her eyes bright with enthusiasm. "Absolutely. In healthcare, the GCN could facilitate better understanding between doctors and patients, improving diagnosis and treatment. In education, it could enhance collaborative learning and foster deeper connections between students and teachers. For national security, it could improve communication and coordination among agencies, potentially preventing conflicts and enhancing crisis response."

Secretary Jameson raised an eyebrow. "Those are impressive applications, Dr. Carter. However, with such powerful technology, there are significant risks. How do you plan to address the ethical and security concerns?"

Emily took a deep breath, ready to tackle the tough questions. "We are fully aware of the potential risks, which is why we have implemented strict protocols to ensure privacy, security, and individual autonomy. Each connection within the GCN is encrypted, and participants have full control over their level of engagement. We are also establishing an independent oversight committee to monitor the network and ensure ethical standards are upheld."

Mr. Patel leaned forward, his expression serious. "What about the potential for rapid deployment and commercialization? There is immense interest from the private sector, and the demand for this technology could be enormous."

Emily's gaze was unwavering. "While we recognize the commercial potential, our primary focus is on ethical development and responsible deployment. We must ensure that the GCN is safe, secure, and beneficial for all users. Rapid commercialization without proper safeguards could lead to misuse and unintended consequences."

Tensions in the room rose as some officials and corporate representatives pushed for faster deployment. Emily could feel the pressure mounting, but she remained resolute. She knew that compromising on ethical standards could jeopardize the entire project.

"Dr. Carter, we understand your concerns," Secretary Jameson said, his tone measured. "But we also need to consider the strategic advantages this technology could provide. How do you propose we balance these interests?"

Emily glanced at Mark, who gave her a reassuring nod. "We propose a phased approach. We can start with controlled pilot programs in specific sectors, closely monitored by the oversight committee. This will allow us to refine the technology, address any issues, and ensure that it is deployed responsibly. We are committed to working with government and industry partners to achieve this balance."

The room fell silent as the officials and representatives considered her proposal. Emily could see the wheels turning in their minds, weighing the potential benefits against the risks.

After a moment, Secretary Jameson spoke. "Your proposal is reasonable, Dr. Carter. We will need to review the details and discuss further, but I believe we can find a path forward that addresses both the opportunities and the concerns."

Emily felt a surge of relief. "Thank you, Secretary Jameson. We are committed to transparency and collaboration. Together, we can ensure that the GCN is developed and deployed in a way that benefits society as a whole."

As the meeting concluded, Emily and Mark exchanged a look of mutual understanding. They had navigated a critical juncture, but the journey was far from over. The support of the government and corporate partners was crucial, but it came with its own set of challenges.

In the quiet of the government office, Emily felt a renewed sense of determination. The vision of a connected world was within reach, but they had to proceed with caution and integrity. With the support of their team and the commitment to ethical development, they were ready to face whatever challenges lay ahead.

"Great job, Emily," Mark said as they left the meeting room. "We're making progress."

Emily smiled, feeling a mix of exhaustion and exhilaration. "Thank you, Mark. Let's keep moving forward. There's still a lot of work to do."

Public Reaction

The town hall was packed, the air buzzing with a mix of excitement and tension. Dr. Emily Carter and Dr. Mark Thompson stood at the front of the room, facing a diverse crowd of community members, activists, and curious onlookers. The announcement of the Global Consciousness Network had sparked intense public interest, and this town hall meeting was an opportunity to address concerns and answer questions directly.

"Thank you all for coming," Emily began, her voice steady despite the butterflies in her stomach. "We're here to discuss the Global Consciousness Network, its potential benefits, and the steps we're taking to ensure it is developed responsibly."

A hand shot up from the middle of the crowd. "Dr. Carter, how can you guarantee that our thoughts and emotions won't be exploited? What safeguards are in place to protect our privacy?" The question came from a middle-aged woman with a determined expression.

Emily nodded, acknowledging the concern. "Privacy and security are our top priorities. Each connection within the GCN is encrypted, and participants have full control over their level of engagement. They can disconnect at any time. Additionally, we are working with cybersecurity experts to develop robust defenses against unauthorized access. We are also establishing an independent oversight committee to monitor the network and ensure ethical standards are upheld."

A young man in the back stood up, his voice filled with skepticism. "But what about the potential for misuse by those in power? How do we know this won't be used to control or manipulate people?"

Emily took a deep breath, ready to address the tough questions. "We recognize the potential risks, which is why we are committed to transparency and accountability. The oversight committee will include representatives from various sectors, including ethics, law, and human rights. Our goal is to create a framework that prioritizes ethical responsibility and safeguards against abuse."

The room buzzed with murmurs as people absorbed her words. Emily could see the mix of emotions on their faces—hope, fear, curiosity, and skepticism. She knew that building trust would take time and effort.

An elderly man raised his hand, his voice gentle but firm. "Dr. Carter, I appreciate your efforts, but I'm worried about the impact on our sense of self. If we're all connected, won't we lose our individuality?"

Emily's heart ached at the genuine concern in his voice. "That's a valid concern, sir. The GCN is designed to enhance communication and empathy, not to erase individuality. Participants can choose the level of connection they are comfortable with, and they retain full control over their thoughts and emotions. Our goal is to foster understanding and collaboration while respecting personal boundaries."

As the questions continued, Emily and Mark did their best to address each one with empathy and clarity. They listened to the fears and hopes of the community, striving to build a bridge of trust and understanding.

In the midst of the discussion, a young woman stood up, her voice trembling with emotion. "My brother has autism, and he struggles to communicate. Could the GCN help people like him connect with others?"

Emily felt a surge of hope. "Yes, the GCN has the potential to help individuals with communication challenges by providing new ways to share thoughts and emotions. We're exploring applications in healthcare and education to support people with diverse needs."

The woman's eyes filled with tears. "Thank you. That gives me hope."

Emily smiled, her heart swelling with gratitude. This was why she had pursued the GCN—to make a positive difference in people's lives. Despite the challenges and the skepticism, moments like this reaffirmed her commitment to the project.

As the town hall meeting drew to a close, Emily addressed the crowd one last time. "Thank you all for your questions and your honesty. We are committed to developing the GCN responsibly and ethically. Your feedback is invaluable, and we will continue to listen and learn from you."

The room erupted in applause, and Emily felt a wave of relief and pride. They had faced the public, addressed their concerns, and taken an important step toward building trust.

After the meeting, Emily and Mark regrouped at the research facility. They reviewed the feedback and discussed the next steps, focusing on refining the GCN and addressing the concerns raised.

"Emily, I think we made a real impact today," Mark said, his voice filled with optimism. "People are starting to see the potential of the GCN."

Emily nodded, feeling a renewed sense of purpose. "Yes, but we have to keep working hard to earn their trust. There's still a lot of work to do."

In the quiet of her office, Emily reflected on the day's events. The journey was far from over, but they were making progress. The vision of a connected world was within reach, and she was determined to see it through.

With the support of her team and the commitment to ethical development, Emily knew they could overcome any challenge. Together, they would make the vision of the Networked Mind a reality.

Moving Forward

The research facility was quiet, the hum of the equipment a comforting backdrop as Dr. Emily Carter and Dr. Mark Thompson sat in Emily's office, surrounded by stacks of reports and data sheets. The whirlwind of the public unveiling had finally settled, leaving them with a mountain of feedback to sift through and a renewed sense of purpose.

Emily leaned back in her chair, rubbing her temples. "It's been a long few days, Mark. But I think we made some real progress."

Mark nodded, his eyes scanning the latest batch of feedback. "We did. The public response was intense, but we managed to address a lot of concerns. Now we need to focus on refining the GCN and implementing the suggestions we've received."

Emily glanced at the clock. It was well past midnight, but she felt a surge of determination. "Let's start with the most pressing issues. The emotional overload some volunteers experienced needs to be addressed immediately. We can't afford any more incidents like Jason's."

Mark tapped a few keys on his tablet, bringing up the relevant data. "I've been thinking about that. We could introduce a tiered connection system, allowing users to gradually increase their level of engagement. It would help them acclimate to the shared experiences without being overwhelmed."

Emily's eyes lit up. "That's a great idea. We should also enhance our encryption protocols to ensure data security. The concerns about privacy and potential misuse are valid, and we need to show that we're taking them seriously."

Mark nodded, making notes on his tablet. "Agreed. And we should expedite the formation of the independent oversight committee. Having a diverse group of experts monitoring the GCN will help build public trust."

Emily felt a wave of gratitude for Mark's unwavering support. "Thank you, Mark. Your insights are invaluable. We're in this together, and I know we can make the GCN a force for good."

They spent the next few hours discussing the next steps, their conversation punctuated by moments of intense focus and bursts of creative energy. Emily felt a renewed sense of purpose as they brainstormed solutions and mapped out their plan.

"Emily, I think we should also consider forming partnerships with educational and healthcare institutions," Mark suggested. "It would allow us to pilot the GCN in controlled environments and gather more data on its impact."

Emily's eyes brightened. "That's a fantastic idea. We can start with a few select institutions and expand from there. It will also help us demonstrate the practical benefits of the GCN."

As the night wore on, Emily and Mark continued to work, their determination unwavering. They knew the road ahead would be challenging, but they were ready to face whatever obstacles came their way. The vision of a connected world, where empathy and understanding transcended barriers, was worth fighting for.

In the quiet of her office, Emily felt a deep sense of resolve. The journey was just beginning, and she was ready to lead the way. With Mark by her side and the support of her team, she knew they could overcome any challenge.

"Great job today, Mark," Emily said, her voice filled with gratitude. "Let's get some rest and start fresh tomorrow. We have a lot of work to do."

Mark smiled, his eyes reflecting the same determination. "Absolutely, Emily. We're just getting started."

As Mark left the office, Emily took a moment to reflect on the day's events. The breakthrough they had achieved was just the beginning. The Global Consciousness Network had the potential to change the world, and she was determined to see it through.

In the stillness of the night, surrounded by the tools of their groundbreaking work, Emily felt a renewed sense of hope. The future was uncertain, but it was also filled with possibility. Together, they would make the vision of the Networked Mind a reality.

5

CHAPTER 4: EARLY ADOPTION

First Adopters

The conference room at the research facility was filled with a palpable sense of anticipation. Dr. Emily Carter and Dr. Mark Thompson stood at the front, facing a group of early adopters who had been carefully selected for their expertise and enthusiasm. The group included scientists, educators, healthcare professionals, and a few forward-thinking business leaders, all eager to explore the potential of the Global Consciousness Network.

"Thank you all for being here," Emily began, her voice steady and welcoming. "Today marks an important milestone for the GCN. You are the first group of early adopters, and your feedback will be crucial as we move forward."

The room was arranged in a semicircle, with each participant seated at a sleek, modern workstation equipped with a neural interface. The screens displayed a series of visualizations and data points, illustrating the capabilities of the GCN.

Mark stepped forward, his demeanor calm and confident. "We'll start with a brief orientation on how to use the technology. The neural interfaces are designed to be intuitive, but we'll walk you through the process step by step."

As Mark explained the technical details, Emily observed the faces of the early adopters. She could see a mix of excitement and apprehension. This was a groundbreaking technology, and while the potential benefits were immense, so were the risks.

Dr. Sarah Mitchell, a renowned neuroscientist, raised her hand. "Dr. Carter, can you elaborate on the practical applications of the GCN in a research setting? How do you envision it enhancing our work?"

Emily smiled, grateful for the thoughtful question. "The GCN can facilitate unprecedented levels of collaboration and data sharing. Researchers can connect their minds to share insights, brainstorm solutions, and even experience each other's thought processes. This could accelerate discoveries and foster a deeper understanding of complex problems."

Sarah nodded, her interest piqued. "That sounds promising. But what about the potential for cognitive overload? How do we ensure that participants aren't overwhelmed by the shared experiences?"

Emily's expression grew serious. "That's a valid concern, Dr. Mitchell. We've implemented a tiered connection system that allows users to gradually increase their level of engagement. This helps them acclimate to the shared experiences without being overwhelmed. Additionally, participants have full control over their connections and can disconnect at any time."

A healthcare professional named Dr. James Lee spoke up next. "In a clinical setting, how can the GCN be used to improve patient care?"

Mark took this question. "The GCN can enhance communication between doctors and patients, allowing for a more empathetic and holistic approach to care. Doctors can gain a deeper understanding of their patients' experiences, leading to more accurate diagnoses and personalized treatment plans. It can also facilitate collaboration among healthcare providers, improving coordination and outcomes."

As the discussion continued, Emily and Mark addressed a range of questions and concerns. Some early adopters expressed excitement about the potential applications, while others voiced their apprehensions about privacy, security, and ethical implications.

A business leader named Karen Foster raised her hand. "What measures are in place to protect the data shared through the GCN? In a corporate environment, data security is paramount."

Emily nodded, understanding the importance of this issue. "Each connection within the GCN is encrypted, and we have implemented robust cybersecurity protocols to protect against unauthorized access. We are also establishing an independent oversight committee to monitor the network and ensure ethical standards are upheld. Your feedback will be crucial in refining these measures."

The room buzzed with conversation as the early adopters discussed the possibilities and challenges of the GCN. Emily felt a surge of pride and responsibility. This was a pivotal moment, and she was determined to guide the project with integrity and transparency.

"Thank you all for your questions and insights," Emily said, bringing the discussion to a close. "Your feedback is invaluable, and we are committed to addressing your concerns as we move forward. Together, we can unlock the full potential of the Global Consciousness Network."

As the meeting adjourned, Emily and Mark exchanged a look of mutual understanding. They had taken an important step, but the journey was far from over. The support and input of the early adopters would be essential in navigating the challenges ahead.

In the quiet of the conference room, Emily felt a renewed sense of purpose. The vision of a connected world was within reach, and with the help of these pioneers, they would make it a reality.

Personal Impact

The aroma of roasted chicken and fresh herbs filled Emily's cozy kitchen as she prepared dinner for her friends. It had been a whirlwind of a week since the public unveiling of the Global Consciousness Network, and she was looking forward to a relaxing evening with familiar faces. The table was set with care, candles flickering softly, casting a warm glow over the room.

Emily's close friend, Lisa, arrived first, carrying a bottle of wine. "Hey, Emily! This smells amazing," Lisa said, giving her a quick hug. "I can't wait to hear all about the GCN. I've been following the news, and it's incredible what you're doing."

"Thanks, Lisa. It's been a lot of work, but we're making progress," Emily replied, smiling. "Let's wait for the others to arrive, and I'll fill you in."

Soon, the rest of the group trickled in—Mark, of course, along with a few other friends who were curious about the GCN. They gathered around the table, chatting and laughing as they served themselves from the spread of dishes Emily had prepared.

As they settled into their meal, the conversation naturally turned to the GCN. "So, Emily, how's it been going with the early adopters?" asked Tom, a software engineer and one of Emily's oldest friends.

Emily took a sip of her wine, considering her response. "It's been a mix of excitement and challenges. The early adopters are enthusiastic, but there are definitely concerns we need to address. Privacy, security, and the emotional impact are all big issues."

Lisa, who was one of the early adopters, nodded thoughtfully. "I've been using the GCN in my classroom, and it's been amazing to see the students connect on a deeper level. But I had a difficult experience the other day. One of my students shared a memory that was really traumatic, and it affected the whole class. It made me realize how powerful and potentially overwhelming this technology can be."

Emily's heart sank. She knew the GCN had the potential to bring people closer together, but she also understood the weight of the responsibility that came with it. "I'm sorry to hear that, Lisa. We're working on ways to moderate the intensity of the connections and provide better support for users. It's a learning process, and your feedback is invaluable."

Mark chimed in, his tone reassuring. "We're also looking into additional training for early adopters, especially in sensitive environments like classrooms and hospitals. It's important that everyone feels prepared to handle these situations."

The conversation continued, with each friend sharing their thoughts and experiences. Emily listened intently, taking mental notes of the feedback and suggestions. She was grateful for their honesty and support, knowing that these discussions were crucial for the GCN's development.

As the evening wore on, the mood lightened, and the group shifted to more casual topics. They laughed and reminisced about old times, the camaraderie providing a much-needed respite from the pressures of their work.

After dinner, Emily and Lisa found themselves alone in the kitchen, washing dishes and chatting quietly. "You know, Emily, despite the challenges, I'm really proud of what you're doing," Lisa said, her voice sincere. "The GCN has so much potential to make a positive impact. Just remember to take care of yourself too."

Emily smiled, touched by her friend's words. "Thanks, Lisa. It means a lot to hear that. And I promise, I'll try to find some balance. It's just hard when there's so much at stake."

Lisa nodded, understanding. "I know. But you're not alone in this. You've got a great team and friends who believe in you. We'll get through the challenges together."

As they finished up in the kitchen, Emily felt a renewed sense of determination. The evening had been a reminder of the personal and emotional implications of the GCN, but it had also reinforced her commitment to the project. She knew there would be obstacles ahead, but with the support of her friends and colleagues, she was ready to face them.

In the quiet of her home, surrounded by the warmth of friendship and the promise of a brighter future, Emily felt a deep sense of purpose. The journey was far from over, but she was more determined than ever to see it through. The vision of a connected world was within reach, and she was ready to lead the way.

Professional Collaboration

The sun was just beginning to rise as Dr. Emily Carter and Dr. Mark Thompson arrived at the hospital, ready to observe the first implementation of the Global Consciousness Network in a healthcare setting. The early morning light filtered through the large windows, casting a warm glow over the bustling lobby. Nurses and doctors moved with purpose, their faces a mix of determination and fatigue.

"Good morning, Dr. Carter, Dr. Thompson," greeted Dr. James Lee, the head of the hospital's neurology department. "We're excited to see how the GCN can enhance our patient care."

"Good morning, Dr. Lee," Emily replied, shaking his hand. "We're eager to see the results as well. Thank you for allowing us to pilot the GCN here."

They made their way to a conference room where a group of doctors and nurses were gathered, ready for a briefing on the GCN. Emily and Mark set up their equipment, the neural interfaces gleaming under the fluorescent lights.

"Thank you all for being here," Emily began, addressing the group. "Today, we'll be using the GCN to facilitate better communication and understanding between healthcare providers and patients. This technology allows for the sharing of thoughts and emotions, which can lead to more accurate diagnoses and personalized treatment plans."

Mark stepped forward to explain the technical aspects. "The neural interfaces are designed to be intuitive and user-friendly. We'll start with a demonstration, and then you'll have the opportunity to use the GCN with your patients."

The first demonstration involved a patient named Maria, who had been experiencing chronic pain that traditional methods had failed to diagnose accurately. Dr. Lee and a nurse named Sarah volunteered to connect with Maria through the GCN.

As the neural interfaces activated, Emily and Mark monitored the data closely. The room fell silent as Dr. Lee and Sarah began to experience Maria's pain and emotions. Their expressions shifted, reflecting the intensity of Maria's experience.

"Dr. Lee, what are you feeling?" Emily asked, her voice gentle.

Dr. Lee took a deep breath, his face etched with concentration. "I can feel the pain radiating from her lower back. It's intense and constant. I also sense her frustration and anxiety about not being able to find relief."

Sarah nodded, her eyes filled with empathy. "It's overwhelming, but it gives us a clearer understanding of what Maria is going through."

Emily watched as Dr. Lee and Sarah disconnected from the GCN, their expressions thoughtful. "This insight can help us tailor a more effective treatment plan for Maria," Dr. Lee said, turning to Emily. "The GCN has the potential to revolutionize patient care."

The demonstration was a success, and the doctors and nurses were eager to try the GCN with their own patients. Emily and Mark moved from room to room, assisting with the connections and gathering feedback.

Later that day, they visited a local school where the GCN was being used in a classroom setting. The students were excited, their faces lighting up as they connected with each other through the neural interfaces. The teacher, Ms. Johnson, guided them through a collaborative project, using the GCN to enhance their communication and teamwork.

"Ms. Johnson, how has the GCN impacted your classroom?" Emily asked, observing the students' interactions.

"It's been incredible," Ms. Johnson replied, her eyes shining with enthusiasm. "The students are more engaged and empathetic. They're able to understand each other's perspectives in a way that wasn't possible before. It's fostering a sense of community and collaboration."

Emily felt a surge of pride and hope. The GCN was making a tangible difference in both healthcare and education, proving its potential to enhance human connection and understanding.

However, not all the feedback was positive. At a corporate office where the GCN was being piloted, Emily and Mark encountered resistance from some employees. They were wary of the technology, concerned about privacy and the potential for misuse.

"I understand your concerns," Emily said, addressing a group of skeptical employees. "The GCN is designed with strict privacy and security measures. Your thoughts and emotions are encrypted, and you have full control over your level of engagement. We're here to support you and address any issues that arise."

Despite her reassurances, some employees remained hesitant. Emily knew that building trust would take time and effort. She and Mark worked closely with the corporate team, providing training and support to help them acclimate to the GCN.

As the day drew to a close, Emily and Mark returned to the research facility, exhausted but optimistic. They had seen the GCN's potential to transform professional environments, but they also recognized the challenges that lay ahead.

"Today was a big step forward," Mark said, his voice filled with determination. "But we have a lot of work to do to address the concerns and refine the technology."

Emily nodded, her mind racing with ideas. "Agreed. We'll take the feedback we've received and use it to improve the GCN. We're on the right path, but we need to keep pushing forward."

In the quiet of the research facility, surrounded by the tools of their groundbreaking work, Emily felt a renewed sense of purpose. The vision of a connected world was within reach, and with the support of their team and the commitment to ethical development, they were ready to face whatever challenges lay ahead.

Public Feedback

The research facility's auditorium was filled with a diverse crowd, eager to share their experiences and opinions about the Global Consciousness Network. Dr. Emily Carter and Dr. Mark Thompson stood at the front, ready to listen and engage with the public. The atmosphere was charged with a mix of excitement, curiosity, and apprehension.

"Thank you all for coming," Emily began, her voice steady and welcoming. "We're here to gather your feedback on the GCN. Your insights are crucial as we continue to refine and develop this technology."

The room was arranged with rows of chairs facing a large screen, where data visualizations and feedback summaries were displayed. Emily and Mark had set up an online forum as well, allowing people to submit their thoughts and questions in real-time.

A hand shot up from the middle of the crowd. "Dr. Carter, my name is Rachel, and I've been using the GCN in my therapy practice. It's been incredibly helpful for understanding my clients' emotions, but I'm concerned about the long-term effects. How do we ensure that this technology doesn't become a crutch?"

Emily nodded, appreciating the thoughtful question. "That's a valid concern, Rachel. The GCN is a tool to enhance communication and empathy, but it should not replace traditional methods of therapy and support. We encourage users to balance their use of the GCN with other forms of interaction and self-care. Ongoing research and feedback from professionals like you will help us develop guidelines to ensure its responsible use."

Another hand went up, this time from a young man in the back. "I'm a high school teacher, and I've noticed that some students are becoming overly reliant on the GCN for social interactions. They're struggling to communicate without it. How do we address this issue?"

Mark stepped forward to answer. "That's an important observation. The GCN is meant to complement, not replace, face-to-face interactions. We need to educate users, especially young people, about the importance of maintaining a balance. We're working on developing educational programs and resources to help integrate the GCN in a healthy and constructive way."

The discussion continued, with a range of opinions and experiences being shared. Some people praised the GCN for its ability to foster deeper connections and understanding, while others raised concerns about privacy, security, and the potential for misuse.

A middle-aged man named Tom stood up, his expression serious. "I've read reports about potential security breaches. How can we be sure that our thoughts and emotions are safe from hackers?"

Emily took a deep breath, ready to address the tough question. "Security is a top priority for us. Each connection within the GCN is encrypted, and we have implemented robust cybersecurity protocols to protect against unauthorized access. We're also working with leading experts in the field to continuously improve our defenses. Additionally, the independent oversight committee will monitor the network to ensure ethical standards are upheld."

The room buzzed with murmurs as people absorbed her words. Emily could see the mix of emotions on their faces—hope, fear, curiosity, and skepticism. She knew that building trust would take time and effort.

A young woman named Jessica raised her hand, her voice filled with emotion. "My brother has been using the GCN to connect with our family. It's helped him feel less isolated, but I'm worried about the emotional intensity. Sometimes it feels overwhelming."

Emily's heart ached at the genuine concern in Jessica's voice. "Thank you for sharing that, Jessica. We're aware of the potential for emotional overload, and we're working on ways to moderate the intensity of the connections. The tiered connection system allows users to gradually increase their level of engagement, helping them acclimate to the shared experiences. Your feedback is crucial in helping us refine these features."

As the feedback session continued, Emily and Mark listened intently, taking notes and addressing each concern with empathy and clarity. They knew that the success of the GCN depended on the trust and support of the public.

After the session, Emily and Mark returned to their office, exhausted but optimistic. They reviewed the feedback and discussed the next steps, focusing on refining the GCN and addressing the concerns raised.

"Emily, I think we made a real impact today," Mark said, his voice filled with determination. "People are starting to see the potential of the GCN, but we need to keep working hard to earn their trust."

Emily nodded, her mind racing with ideas. "Agreed. We'll take the feedback we've received and use it to improve the GCN. We're on the right path, but we need to keep pushing forward."

In the quiet of the research facility, surrounded by the tools of their groundbreaking work, Emily felt a renewed sense of purpose. The vision of a connected world was within reach, and with the support of their team and the commitment to ethical development, they were ready to face whatever challenges lay ahead.

Moving Forward

The research facility was quiet, the hum of the equipment a familiar backdrop as Dr. Emily Carter and Dr. Mark Thompson sat in Emily's office, surrounded by stacks of reports and data sheets. The whirlwind of the public unveiling and the feedback sessions had finally settled, leaving them with a mountain of insights to sift through and a renewed sense of purpose.

Emily leaned back in her chair, rubbing her temples. "It's been a long few days, Mark. But I think we made some real progress."

Mark nodded, his eyes scanning the latest batch of feedback. "We did. The public response was intense, but we managed to address a lot of concerns. Now we need to focus on refining the GCN and implementing the suggestions we've received."

Emily glanced at the clock. It was well past midnight, but she felt a surge of determination. "Let's start with the most pressing issues. The emotional overload some volunteers experienced needs to be addressed immediately. We can't afford any more incidents like Jason's."

Mark tapped a few keys on his tablet, bringing up the relevant data. "I've been thinking about that. We could introduce a tiered connection system, allowing users to gradually increase their level of engagement. It would help them acclimate to the shared experiences without being overwhelmed."

Emily's eyes lit up. "That's a great idea. We should also enhance our encryption protocols to ensure data security. The concerns about privacy and potential misuse are valid, and we need to show that we're taking them seriously."

Mark nodded, making notes on his tablet. "Agreed. And we should expedite the formation of the independent oversight committee. Having a diverse group of experts monitoring the GCN will help build public trust."

Emily felt a wave of gratitude for Mark's unwavering support. "Thank you, Mark. Your insights are invaluable. We're in this together, and I know we can make the GCN a force for good."

They spent the next few hours discussing the next steps, their conversation punctuated by moments of intense focus and bursts of creative energy. Emily felt a renewed sense of purpose as they brainstormed solutions and mapped out their plan.

"Emily, I think we should also consider forming partnerships with educational and healthcare institutions," Mark suggested. "It would allow us to pilot the GCN in controlled environments and gather more data on its impact."

Emily's eyes brightened. "That's a fantastic idea. We can start with a few select institutions and expand from there. It will also help us demonstrate the practical benefits of the GCN."

As the night wore on, Emily and Mark continued to work, their determination unwavering. They knew the road ahead would be challenging, but they were ready to face whatever obstacles came their way. The vision of a connected world, where empathy and understanding transcended barriers, was worth fighting for.

In the quiet of her office, Emily felt a deep sense of resolve. The journey was just beginning, and she was ready to lead the way. With Mark by her side and the support of her team, she knew they could overcome any challenge.

"Great job today, Mark," Emily said, her voice filled with gratitude. "Let's get some rest and start fresh tomorrow. We have a lot of work to do."

Mark smiled, his eyes reflecting the same determination. "Absolutely, Emily. We're just getting started."

As Mark left the office, Emily took a moment to reflect on the day's events. The breakthrough they had achieved was just the beginning. The Global Consciousness Network had the potential to change the world, and she was determined to see it through.

In the stillness of the night, surrounded by the tools of their groundbreaking work, Emily felt a renewed sense of hope. The future was uncertain, but it was also filled with possibility. Together, they would make the vision of the Networked Mind a reality.

6

CHAPTER 5: UNINTENDED CONSEQUENCES

Rising Concerns

The conference room at the research facility was filled with a tense silence as Dr. Emily Carter and her team gathered to discuss the latest reports on the Global Consciousness Network. The room, usually a hub of excitement and innovation, now felt heavy with the weight of growing concerns. Emily stood at the head of the table, her expression serious as she looked at the faces of her dedicated team.

"Thank you all for coming on such short notice," Emily began, her voice steady but tinged with worry. "We've been receiving increasing reports of negative side effects from the GCN. Mental overload, loss of individuality, and emotional distress are among the most concerning issues."

Dr. Mark Thompson, seated next to Emily, nodded in agreement. "We've analyzed the data, and it's clear that these problems are not isolated incidents. We need to address them immediately."

The large screen at the front of the room displayed graphs and charts, illustrating the troubling trends. Emily clicked through the slides, highlighting the key points. "As you can see, the frequency of these side effects has been rising steadily. We need to understand why this is happening and find solutions."

Dr. Sarah Mitchell, a neuroscientist who had been instrumental in developing the GCN, spoke up. "One possible explanation is that the neural interfaces are too powerful. The intensity of the shared experiences might be overwhelming for some users."

Dr. James Lee, head of the cybersecurity team, added, "We've also detected potential vulnerabilities in the system. If these are being exploited, it could be exacerbating the problem."

Emily felt a knot of guilt tighten in her stomach. She had envisioned the GCN as a tool for empathy and connection, but the unintended consequences were becoming increasingly apparent. "We need to address both the technical and psychological aspects of this issue. Let's brainstorm potential solutions."

The room buzzed with activity as the team members discussed various ideas. Some suggested reducing the intensity of the neural connections, while others proposed enhancing the security protocols to prevent potential breaches. Emily listened intently, taking notes and weighing the pros and cons of each suggestion.

Dr. Mitchell leaned forward, her expression thoughtful. "What if we implement a tiered connection system? Users could start with lower levels of engagement and gradually increase as they become more comfortable. It would help them acclimate to the shared experiences without being overwhelmed."

Emily nodded, considering the idea. "That could work. It would give users more control over their experience and reduce the risk of mental overload."

Dr. Lee added, "We should also enhance our encryption protocols and conduct a thorough security audit. If there are vulnerabilities, we need to identify and fix them immediately."

As the discussion continued, tensions began to rise. Some team members were frustrated by the setbacks, while others were anxious about the potential fallout. Emily could feel the weight of responsibility pressing down on her. She had to find a way to navigate these challenges and protect the integrity of the GCN.

"Everyone, I understand your concerns," Emily said, her voice firm but compassionate. "This is a difficult situation, but we need to stay focused and work together. Our priority is to ensure the safety and well-being of our users. Let's develop a comprehensive plan to address these issues."

The team members nodded, their expressions resolute. They knew the road ahead would be challenging, but they were committed to finding solutions. Emily felt a surge of gratitude for their dedication and support.

As the meeting drew to a close, Emily summarized the key action points. "We'll implement the tiered connection system and enhance our security protocols. Dr. Mitchell, please lead the effort on the psychological aspects, and Dr. Lee, focus on the cybersecurity measures. We'll reconvene in a week to review our progress."

The team dispersed, leaving Emily and Mark alone in the conference room. Mark placed a reassuring hand on her shoulder. "We'll get through this, Emily. We've faced challenges before, and we've always found a way."

Emily nodded, her resolve strengthening. "I know, Mark. We have to. The vision of the GCN is too important to give up on. We'll find a way to make it work."

In the quiet of the conference room, surrounded by the tools of their groundbreaking work, Emily felt a renewed sense of determination. The journey was far from over, but with the support of her team and the commitment to ethical development, she was ready to face whatever challenges lay ahead. Together, they would find a way to overcome the unintended consequences and realize the full potential of the Networked Mind.

Public Backlash

The sun was setting, casting long shadows across the research facility as Dr. Emily Carter and Dr. Mark Thompson stood by the large windows, watching the growing crowd outside. Protesters had gathered, their signs and chants echoing through the air. The once-quiet facility was now the epicenter of a heated public debate.

"Emily, we need to address this," Mark said, his voice filled with concern. "The negative side effects of the GCN are causing real fear. We have to find a way to calm the situation."

Emily nodded, her heart heavy with the weight of responsibility. "I know, Mark. Let's go out there and talk to them. We need to show that we're listening and that we're committed to finding solutions."

They made their way to the front entrance, where security personnel were trying to keep the crowd at bay. The protesters' faces were a mix of anger, fear, and desperation. Emily took a deep breath and stepped forward, raising her hands to signal for attention.

"Please, everyone, can I have your attention?" she called out, her voice steady but loud enough to be heard over the noise. "I'm Dr. Emily Carter, and this is Dr. Mark Thompson. We understand your concerns, and we're here to listen."

A woman in the front of the crowd, holding a sign that read "Protect Our Minds," stepped forward. "Dr. Carter, my daughter has been using the GCN, and she's been experiencing severe anxiety and emotional distress. What are you doing to fix this?"

Emily's heart ached at the woman's words. "I'm so sorry to hear that. We're aware of the issues, and we're working tirelessly to address them. We've already started implementing a tiered connection system to help users acclimate gradually. We're also enhancing our security protocols to protect against any potential breaches."

Another protester, a young man with a determined expression, shouted, "How can we trust you? You've created something that can invade our minds. How do we know it won't be used against us?"

Emily felt the weight of his accusation. "I understand your fear. The GCN was created to foster empathy and understanding, not to invade privacy. We're establishing an independent oversight committee to ensure that the technology is used ethically and responsibly. Your feedback is crucial in helping us improve and safeguard the GCN."

The crowd murmured, some people nodding in cautious agreement while others remained skeptical. Emily knew that building trust would take time and consistent effort.

Mark stepped forward, his voice calm and reassuring. "We are committed to transparency and accountability. We invite you to participate in our feedback sessions and share your experiences. Together, we can make the GCN a tool for positive change."

As the protesters began to disperse, Emily and Mark returned to the facility, their minds racing with the challenges ahead. They knew that the public backlash was a serious threat to the project's future, but they were determined to address the concerns and find solutions.

Later that evening, Emily sat in her office, scrolling through online forums filled with heated debates about the GCN. Some users praised the technology for its potential to connect people, while others voiced fears about privacy and mental health.

One post caught her eye: "The GCN is a double-edged sword. It has the power to bring us closer together, but it also has the potential to tear us apart. We need to hold the creators accountable and ensure that it's used responsibly."

Emily sighed, feeling the weight of the responsibility on her shoulders. She knew that the journey ahead would be fraught with challenges, but she was committed to seeing it through.

Mark knocked on her door, his expression serious. "Emily, we've received more reports of negative side effects. We need to address these issues urgently."

Emily nodded, her resolve strengthening. "Let's gather the team and develop a comprehensive plan. We need to enhance user support, improve the technology, and rebuild public trust."

As they worked late into the night, Emily felt a renewed sense of determination. The vision of a connected world was within reach, but it required careful navigation and unwavering commitment to ethical development.

In the quiet of the research facility, surrounded by the tools of their groundbreaking work, Emily and Mark forged ahead, driven by the hope of creating a better, more connected future. They knew that the road would be difficult, but they were ready to face whatever challenges lay ahead. Together, they would find a way to overcome the unintended consequences and realize the full potential of the Networked Mind.

Personal Struggles

The night was quiet, the only sound the soft ticking of the clock on the wall. Dr. Emily Carter sat in her living room, the glow from the fireplace casting flickering shadows across the room. She cradled a cup of tea in her hands, her mind heavy with the weight of the day's events. The public backlash against the Global Consciousness Network was growing, and the reports of negative side effects were becoming harder to ignore.

A knock on the door broke the silence. Emily set her cup down and went to answer it, finding her estranged brother, Alex, standing on the doorstep. His expression was a mix of concern and hesitation.

"Alex, what are you doing here?" Emily asked, surprised but not unwelcome.

"I heard about the protests," Alex replied, stepping inside. "I thought you might need someone to talk to."

Emily closed the door behind him and led him to the living room. They sat down, the fire providing a comforting warmth. For a moment, they sat in silence, the unspoken tension between them palpable.

"How have you been?" Emily finally asked, breaking the silence.

Alex shrugged. "I've been okay. Busy with work. But I've been following the news about the GCN. It sounds like you're facing some serious challenges."

Emily sighed, her shoulders slumping. "You have no idea. The negative side effects, the public backlash... It's all becoming overwhelming. I feel like I'm failing."

Alex looked at her, his eyes filled with empathy. "You're not failing, Emily. You're dealing with something incredibly complex. But you need to remember why you started this project in the first place."

Emily felt a lump form in her throat. "I wanted to create something that would bring people closer together, help them understand each other. But now it feels like it's causing more harm than good."

Alex reached out and took her hand, his touch grounding her. "Every innovation comes with challenges. The important thing is how you respond to them. You have the power to make things right."

Emily looked at her brother, seeing the sincerity in his eyes. "I just don't know if I can handle it all. The responsibility, the guilt... It's too much."

Alex squeezed her hand. "You don't have to do it alone. You have a team, and you have people who believe in you. And you have me, even if we haven't always seen eye to eye."

Emily felt tears welling up in her eyes. "Thank you, Alex. I needed to hear that."

They sat in silence for a while, the fire crackling softly. Emily felt a sense of relief, knowing that she wasn't alone in this struggle. She had her brother's support, and that meant more than she could express.

"Do you remember when we were kids, and we used to build those elaborate Lego structures?" Alex asked, a hint of a smile on his lips.

Emily chuckled, wiping away a tear. "Yeah, we always tried to outdo each other. But we also worked together to make something amazing."

Alex nodded. "Exactly. You have that same spirit now. You can face these challenges and find a way to make the GCN work. Just take it one step at a time."

Emily felt a renewed sense of determination. "You're right. I can't let the setbacks define the project. I need to focus on finding solutions and making things right."

Alex smiled, his eyes filled with pride. "That's the Emily I know. You're stronger than you think."

As the night wore on, they talked about their childhood, their dreams, and the challenges they had faced. Emily felt a sense of healing, the old wounds between them beginning to mend. She knew that the road ahead would be difficult, but she also knew that she had the strength and support to navigate it.

When Alex finally left, Emily felt a renewed sense of purpose. She returned to her desk, her mind clear and focused. She began drafting a plan to address the issues with the GCN, determined to make things right.

In the quiet of her home, surrounded by the warmth of the fire and the memories of her conversation with Alex, Emily felt a deep sense of resolve. The journey was far from over, but she was ready to face whatever challenges lay ahead. With the support of her team and the commitment to ethical development, she would find a way to overcome the unintended consequences and realize the full potential of the Networked Mind.

The Hacker Threat

The research facility was a hive of activity as the cybersecurity team worked around the clock to counteract the latest threat. Dr. Emily Carter and Dr. Mark Thompson stood in the cybersecurity lab, the air thick with tension. The screens displayed a barrage of data, flashing alerts, and lines of code as the team battled to secure the Global Consciousness Network from a coordinated hacker attack.

"Emily, we've identified the source of the breach," said Dr. James Lee, the head of the cybersecurity team. His face was etched with concentration as he typed furiously on his keyboard. "It's a sophisticated attack, likely from a well-funded group. They're exploiting vulnerabilities we didn't even know existed."

Emily felt a chill run down her spine. The GCN was supposed to be a beacon of hope and connection, but now it was under siege. "What can we do to stop them, James?"

"We're deploying countermeasures and patching the vulnerabilities as quickly as we can," James replied, his eyes never leaving the screen. "But it's a race against time. They're trying to access the core of the network, and if they succeed, they could cause widespread chaos."

Mark stepped forward, his expression grim. "We need to inform the public about the breach and reassure them that we're doing everything possible to secure the network. Transparency is key to maintaining trust."

Emily nodded, her mind racing. "Agreed. I'll draft a statement and coordinate with our communications team. We need to stay ahead of this and show that we're in control."

As Emily and Mark left the lab, the weight of the situation pressed heavily on Emily's shoulders. She knew that the integrity of the GCN was at stake, and the consequences of failure were unthinkable.

In her office, Emily quickly drafted a statement, outlining the steps they were taking to secure the network and urging users to remain vigilant. She sent it to the communications team, who began disseminating the information through various channels.

"Emily, we need to address the media as well," Mark said, entering her office. "A press conference will help us reach a wider audience and answer any questions directly."

Emily took a deep breath, steeling herself for the task ahead. "Let's do it. We need to show that we're taking this seriously and that we're committed to protecting our users."

The press conference room was filled with reporters, their cameras and microphones ready. Emily and Mark stood at the podium, the bright lights casting harsh shadows on their faces.

"Good afternoon," Emily began, her voice steady but firm. "We have detected a coordinated hacker attack on the Global Consciousness Network. Our cybersecurity team is working tirelessly to counteract the threat and secure the network. We are taking every possible measure to protect our users and ensure the integrity of the GCN."

A reporter raised his hand. "Dr. Carter, can you provide more details about the nature of the attack and the potential risks to users?"

Emily nodded. "The attackers are exploiting previously unknown vulnerabilities in the network. Their goal appears to be to access the core of the GCN, which could lead to significant disruptions. We are deploying countermeasures and patching the vulnerabilities as quickly as possible. We urge all users to remain vigilant and report any suspicious activity."

Another reporter asked, "What steps are you taking to prevent future attacks?"

Mark stepped in to answer. "We are conducting a comprehensive security audit and enhancing our encryption protocols. Additionally, we are working with leading cybersecurity experts to develop more robust defenses. The independent oversight committee will also play a crucial role in monitoring the network and ensuring ethical standards are upheld."

The press conference continued, with Emily and Mark addressing a range of questions and concerns. They knew that transparency and communication were essential to maintaining public trust.

As the press conference concluded, Emily felt a mix of exhaustion and determination. The hacker threat was a serious challenge, but she was committed to protecting the GCN and its users.

Back in the cybersecurity lab, the team was making progress. "We've managed to block several of their access points," James reported. "But they're persistent. We need to stay vigilant."

Emily nodded, her resolve strengthening. "Keep up the good work, James. We're counting on you."

In the quiet of the lab, surrounded by the hum of computers and the focused determination of her team, Emily felt a renewed sense of purpose. The journey was far from over, but with the support of her team and the commitment to ethical development, she was ready to face whatever challenges lay ahead. Together, they would find a way to overcome the hacker threat and realize the full potential of the Networked Mind.

A Plan for Redemption

The research facility was quiet, the hum of the equipment a familiar backdrop as Dr. Emily Carter and Dr. Mark Thompson sat in Emily's office, surrounded by stacks of reports and data sheets. The recent hacker attack had been a wake-up call, and the team was now focused on developing a comprehensive plan to address the issues with the Global Consciousness Network.

Emily leaned back in her chair, her eyes scanning the room. "We've managed to counteract the immediate threat, but we need a long-term solution. We can't afford any more breaches or negative side effects."

Mark nodded, his expression serious. "Agreed. We need to enhance our security measures and provide better support for our users. The tiered connection system is a good start, but we need to do more."

Emily glanced at the whiteboard, which was covered in notes and diagrams. "Let's break this down into actionable steps. First, we need to conduct a thorough security audit. Identify any remaining vulnerabilities and patch them immediately."

Mark made a note on his tablet. "I'll coordinate with James and the cybersecurity team. We'll also bring in external experts to ensure we haven't missed anything."

"Next, we need to improve user control," Emily continued. "The tiered connection system should help, but we also need to provide more options for users to customize their experience. They should be able to adjust the intensity of the connections and set boundaries for what they share."

Mark nodded. "We can develop a user-friendly interface that allows for these adjustments. It will give users more autonomy and help prevent emotional overload."

Emily felt a surge of determination. "We also need to enhance our support systems. Users should have access to mental health resources and support groups. We can partner with therapists and counselors to provide guidance and assistance."

Mark smiled, his eyes reflecting the same resolve. "That's a great idea. We can create a network of professionals who are trained to help users navigate their experiences with the GCN."

As they continued to brainstorm, Emily felt a renewed sense of purpose. The challenges they faced were daunting, but she was confident that they could overcome them with the right approach.

"Emily, we should also focus on rebuilding public trust," Mark said. "Transparency is key. We need to keep the public informed about our progress and the steps we're taking to address their concerns."

Emily nodded. "Agreed. We'll hold regular press conferences and update our website with detailed information. We should also invite users to participate in feedback sessions and involve them in the development process."

Mark made another note. "I'll coordinate with the communications team. We need to be proactive and show that we're committed to making the GCN safe and beneficial for everyone."

As the night wore on, Emily and Mark continued to work, their determination unwavering. They knew that the road ahead would be challenging, but they were ready to face whatever obstacles came their way. The vision of a connected world, where empathy and understanding transcended barriers, was worth fighting for.

In the quiet of her office, surrounded by the tools of their groundbreaking work, Emily felt a deep sense of resolve. The journey was far from over, but with the support of her team and the commitment to ethical development, she was ready to lead the way.

"Great job today, Mark," Emily said, her voice filled with gratitude. "Let's get some rest and start fresh tomorrow. We have a lot of work to do."

Mark smiled, his eyes reflecting the same determination. "Absolutely, Emily. We're just getting started."

As Mark left the office, Emily took a moment to reflect on the day's events. The breakthrough they had achieved was just the beginning. The Global Consciousness Network had the potential to change the world, and she was determined to see it through.

In the stillness of the night, surrounded by the promise of a brighter future, Emily felt a renewed sense of hope. Together, they would make the vision of the Networked Mind a reality.

7

CHAPTER 6: THE DARK SIDE

The Hacker Group

The warehouse was dimly lit, the air thick with the scent of dust and oil. Dr. Emily Carter and Dr. Mark Thompson moved cautiously through the shadows, their footsteps echoing softly on the concrete floor. They had managed to infiltrate the headquarters of the hacker group that had been exploiting the vulnerabilities in the Global Consciousness Network. The stakes were high, and the tension was palpable.

"Stay close," Mark whispered, his eyes scanning the darkened space for any signs of movement. "We need to find their main server room and gather as much information as we can."

Emily nodded, her heart pounding in her chest. She could feel the weight of the situation pressing down on her. The GCN was her creation, and it was being used against her vision of a connected and empathetic world. She had to understand the hackers' motives and find a way to stop them.

They moved deeper into the warehouse, passing rows of old machinery and stacks of crates. The faint glow of computer screens guided them toward the back of the building, where they found a makeshift command center. Several hackers were hunched over their keyboards, their faces illuminated by the eerie blue light of the monitors.

Emily and Mark exchanged a glance, then slipped into the shadows to observe. The hackers were engrossed in their work, their fingers flying over the keys as they executed complex commands. Emily strained to hear their conversation, hoping to glean some insight into their plans.

"This latest breach should send a clear message," one of the hackers said, his voice low and determined. "The GCN is a tool for control and manipulation. We need to expose its dangers and bring it down."

Another hacker nodded in agreement. "People need to understand that their thoughts and emotions are not safe. The GCN is a threat to individual freedom and privacy."

Emily felt a chill run down her spine. The hackers saw the GCN as a weapon, a means of control rather than a tool for connection. She had to find a way to change their perception and protect the integrity of her creation.

Mark nudged her gently, pointing to a door at the far end of the room. "That looks like the server room. We need to get in there and see what they're planning."

They waited for a moment when the hackers were distracted, then slipped through the door and into the server room. The hum of the machines filled the air, and the walls were lined with racks of servers, their lights blinking rhythmically.

Emily pulled out a small device from her pocket and connected it to one of the servers. "This should give us access to their files. We need to find out how they're breaching the GCN and what their next move is."

Mark kept watch at the door, his eyes darting back and forth. "Hurry, Emily. We don't have much time."

Emily's fingers flew over the keys as she navigated through the hackers' files. She found detailed plans for future attacks, lists of vulnerabilities in the GCN, and communications between the hackers. Her heart sank as she realized the extent of their knowledge and the sophistication of their operations.

"We need to get this information back to the team," Emily said, her voice tense. "They know more about the GCN's weaknesses than we do. We have to stay one step ahead."

Just as she finished downloading the files, the door burst open, and the hackers stormed in. "What are you doing here?" one of them shouted, his eyes blazing with anger.

Emily and Mark exchanged a quick glance, then bolted for the exit. They sprinted through the warehouse, the hackers hot on their heels. Emily's heart pounded in her chest as she pushed herself to run faster, the weight of the stolen information heavy in her pocket.

They burst out into the night, the cool air a stark contrast to the stifling heat of the warehouse. Emily and Mark didn't stop running until they reached their car, breathless and exhilarated.

"That was close," Mark said, his voice shaky. "But we got what we needed."

Emily nodded, her mind racing with the implications of what they had discovered. "We need to get back to the facility and analyze this data. The hackers are more organized and determined than we thought. We have to be ready for whatever they throw at us next."

As they drove back to the research facility, Emily felt a renewed sense of determination. The journey was far from over, but with the support of her team and the commitment to ethical development, she was ready to face whatever challenges lay ahead. Together, they would find a way to overcome the dark side of the GCN and realize the full potential of the Networked Mind.

Internal Strife

The research facility's secure meeting room was filled with a tense silence as Dr. Emily Carter and Dr. Mark Thompson returned from their infiltration of the hacker group's headquarters. The team had been waiting anxiously for their arrival, and now they gathered around the large conference table, their faces etched with concern and anticipation.

Emily placed a USB drive on the table, the weight of its contents heavy in the room. "We managed to gather a significant amount of information about the hacker group," she began, her voice steady but strained. "They see the GCN as a tool for control and manipulation, and they're determined to bring it down."

Dr. Sarah Mitchell, the neuroscientist who had been instrumental in developing the GCN, leaned forward. "What did you find out about their plans?"

Emily took a deep breath. "They have detailed knowledge of the GCN's vulnerabilities. Their attacks are sophisticated and well-coordinated. They believe that by exposing the GCN's weaknesses, they can turn public opinion against it and force us to shut it down."

The room erupted in a flurry of voices as the team members reacted to the news. Some were shocked, others angry, and a few were visibly shaken. Emily raised her hand to call for silence.

"We need to stay focused," she said firmly. "We have to address these vulnerabilities and strengthen our defenses. But we also need to consider the ethical implications of continuing with the GCN in its current form."

Dr. James Lee, head of the cybersecurity team, spoke up. "We can enhance our encryption protocols and deploy additional security measures. But we need to act quickly. The hackers are relentless, and we can't afford any more breaches."

Dr. Mitchell nodded in agreement. "We also need to address the psychological impact on users. The tiered connection system is a good start, but we need to provide more support and resources to help users navigate their experiences."

As the discussion continued, tensions began to rise. Some team members advocated for shutting down the GCN temporarily to prevent further exploitation, while others argued that doing so would be a victory for the hackers and a setback for their vision of a connected world.

Dr. Karen Foster, a psychologist on the team, voiced her concerns. "Shutting down the GCN might be the safest option for now. We need to prioritize the well-being of our users and ensure that we're not causing more harm than good."

Emily felt a knot of guilt tighten in her stomach. She had always believed in the potential of the GCN to foster empathy and understanding, but the unintended consequences were becoming increasingly apparent. "I understand your concerns, Karen. But shutting down the GCN would also mean abandoning the progress we've made. We need to find a balance."

Mark, who had been listening quietly, finally spoke up. "We can't let fear dictate our actions. The GCN has the potential to change the world for the better, but we need to address the issues head-on. We need to be transparent with the public and show them that we're committed to making the GCN safe and beneficial."

The room fell silent as the team absorbed Mark's words. Emily could see the conflict in their eyes, the struggle between their dedication to the project and their fear of the risks.

"We need to make a decision," Emily said, her voice resolute. "We will enhance our security measures and provide better support for our users. We will also hold a press conference to inform the public about the hacker group and the steps we're taking to protect the GCN. Transparency is key to maintaining trust."

The team members nodded, their expressions a mix of determination and apprehension. They knew the road ahead would be challenging, but they were committed to finding solutions.

As the meeting adjourned, Emily and Mark stayed behind, the weight of the responsibility pressing down on them. "We have to stay strong, Emily," Mark said, his voice filled with resolve. "We can't let the hackers win."

Emily nodded, her mind racing with the challenges they faced. "I know, Mark. We'll find a way to overcome this. The vision of the GCN is too important to give up on."

In the quiet of the meeting room, surrounded by the tools of their groundbreaking work, Emily felt a renewed sense of determination. The journey was far from over, but with the support of her team and the commitment to ethical development, she was ready to face whatever challenges lay ahead. Together, they would find a way to overcome the dark side of the GCN and realize the full potential of the Networked Mind.

The Public Reveal

The press conference room at the research facility was packed with reporters, their cameras and microphones poised to capture every word. Dr. Emily Carter and Dr. Mark Thompson stood at the podium, the bright lights casting harsh shadows on their faces. The atmosphere was charged with anticipation and tension, the weight of the recent hacker attacks heavy in the air.

Emily took a deep breath, her heart pounding in her chest. She knew that this moment was crucial for the future of the Global Consciousness Network. They had to be transparent and honest, addressing the public's concerns head-on.

"Good afternoon," Emily began, her voice steady but firm. "Thank you all for being here. We have called this press conference to address the recent security breaches and the actions we are taking to protect the Global Consciousness Network and its users."

The room fell silent, the reporters hanging on her every word. Emily glanced at Mark, who gave her a reassuring nod.

"Over the past few weeks, we have been targeted by a sophisticated hacker group," Emily continued. "These individuals have exploited vulnerabilities in the GCN, causing significant disruptions and raising serious concerns about the safety and security of the network."

She paused, letting the gravity of her words sink in. "We have identified the group responsible for these attacks. They believe that the GCN is a tool for control and manipulation, and they are determined to bring it down. We understand their concerns, but we strongly disagree with their methods and their assessment of the GCN's potential."

A reporter raised his hand, his expression serious. "Dr. Carter, can you provide more details about the nature of these attacks and the steps you are taking to prevent future breaches?"

Emily nodded. "The hackers have been exploiting previously unknown vulnerabilities in the network. Their goal is to access the core of the GCN, which could lead to significant disruptions. We are deploying countermeasures and patching the vulnerabilities as quickly as possible. Additionally, we are conducting a comprehensive security audit and enhancing our encryption protocols to protect against future attacks."

Another reporter asked, "What about the psychological impact on users? There have been reports of mental overload and emotional distress. How are you addressing these issues?"

Mark stepped forward to answer. "We are implementing a tiered connection system that allows users to gradually increase their level of engagement. This helps them acclimate to the shared experiences without being overwhelmed. We are also providing more support and resources, including access to mental health professionals and support groups, to help users navigate their experiences with the GCN."

The room buzzed with murmurs as the reporters absorbed their words. Emily could see the mix of emotions on their faces—fear, curiosity, skepticism, and a glimmer of hope.

A young woman in the front row raised her hand. "Dr. Carter, how can you reassure the public that the GCN is safe and beneficial, given the recent attacks and negative side effects?"

Emily took a deep breath, her resolve strengthening. "We understand the concerns, and we are committed to addressing them. The GCN was created to foster empathy and understanding, and we believe in its potential to bring people closer together. We are taking every possible measure to ensure its safety and integrity. Transparency and accountability are key, and we will continue to keep the public informed about our progress and the steps we are taking to protect the GCN."

The press conference continued, with Emily and Mark addressing a range of questions and concerns. They knew that rebuilding public trust would take time and consistent effort, but they were determined to show their commitment to making the GCN safe and beneficial for everyone.

As the press conference drew to a close, Emily felt a mix of exhaustion and determination. They had faced the public, acknowledged the challenges, and outlined their plan to address them. It was a crucial step forward, but the journey was far from over.

Back in her office, Emily sat down at her desk, her mind racing with the events of the day. She knew that the road ahead would be difficult, but she was ready to face whatever challenges lay ahead. With the support of her team and the commitment to ethical development, she was determined to protect the GCN and realize its full potential.

Mark entered the office, his expression serious but hopeful. "You did great today, Emily. We made it clear that we're taking this seriously and that we're committed to finding solutions."

Emily smiled, feeling a renewed sense of purpose. "Thank you, Mark. We have a lot of work to do, but I believe in the vision of the GCN. Together, we'll find a way to overcome these challenges and create a better, more connected world."

In the quiet of her office, surrounded by the tools of their groundbreaking work, Emily felt a deep sense of resolve. The journey was far from over, but with the support of her team and the commitment to ethical development, she was ready to lead the way. Together, they would make the vision of the Networked Mind a reality.

The Counterattack

The research facility was a flurry of activity as the cybersecurity team worked tirelessly to fend off the latest attack. The hacker group had launched a coordinated counterattack, aiming to disrupt the Global Consciousness Network and incite widespread panic. Dr. Emily Carter and Dr. Mark Thompson stood in the cybersecurity lab, their faces illuminated by the glow of multiple monitors displaying real-time data and alerts.

"Emily, the hackers are targeting the core of the GCN again," Dr. James Lee reported, his fingers flying over the keyboard. "They're using a new method to bypass our defenses. We need to act fast."

Emily's heart pounded as she watched the data streams. "What can we do to stop them, James?"

"We're deploying additional countermeasures and rerouting traffic to minimize the impact," James replied, his voice tense but focused. "But we need to identify their entry points and shut them down."

Mark stepped forward, his expression resolute. "Emily, we need to coordinate our response. I'll handle the communication with the public and our partners. You focus on leading the team here."

Emily nodded, her mind racing with the gravity of the situation. "Let's do it. We can't let them succeed."

As Mark left to manage the external communications, Emily turned her attention to the team. "Everyone, listen up! We need to stay focused and work together. Identify the entry points and shut them down. Deploy all available countermeasures. We have to protect the GCN at all costs."

The team sprang into action, their movements precise and coordinated. Emily moved from station to station, offering guidance and support. The room was filled with the hum of computers and the rapid clicking of keyboards, punctuated by the occasional beep of an alert.

"Emily, we've identified one of the main entry points," James called out. "It's a vulnerability in the encryption protocol. We're working on patching it now."

"Good work, James," Emily replied, her voice steady. "Keep me updated on your progress."

As the minutes ticked by, the intensity of the attack increased. The hackers were relentless, their methods becoming more sophisticated and aggressive. Emily could feel the strain on her team, but she knew they couldn't afford to falter.

"Emily, we're seeing unusual activity in the user data," one of the analysts reported. "It looks like the hackers are trying to manipulate the connections to cause emotional distress."

Emily's heart sank. The hackers were not only targeting the network but also the users themselves. "We need to warn the users and provide support. Activate the emergency protocols and send out alerts."

The team worked swiftly to implement the emergency measures, sending out notifications to users and providing resources for mental health support. Emily felt a surge of determination. They had to protect the users and the integrity of the GCN.

"James, how's the patch coming along?" Emily asked, her eyes fixed on the monitor.

"We're almost there," James replied, his voice strained. "Just a few more minutes."

Emily's mind raced with the implications of the attack. The hackers were determined to undermine the GCN, but she couldn't let them succeed. She had to stay focused and lead her team through the crisis.

"Emily, we've patched the vulnerability," James announced. "But the hackers are still trying to find other entry points."

"Keep monitoring the network and deploy additional defenses," Emily instructed. "We need to stay one step ahead."

As the hours passed, the team continued to fend off the attack, their determination unwavering. Emily felt a mix of exhaustion and resolve. They were making progress, but the battle was far from over.

"Emily, we've managed to block several of their access points," James reported. "The intensity of the attack is decreasing."

Emily let out a sigh of relief. "Great work, everyone. Keep monitoring the network and stay vigilant. We can't let our guard down."

As the immediate threat subsided, Emily and her team took a moment to regroup. The room was filled with a sense of cautious optimism. They had faced a significant challenge and emerged stronger.

Mark returned to the lab, his expression a mix of relief and determination. "The public response has been positive. People appreciate our transparency and the steps we're taking to protect the GCN."

Emily smiled, feeling a renewed sense of purpose. "Thank you, Mark. We still have a lot of work to do, but we're on the right path."

In the quiet of the cybersecurity lab, surrounded by the tools of their groundbreaking work, Emily felt a deep sense of resolve. The journey was far from over, but with the support of her team and the commitment to ethical development, she was ready to face whatever challenges lay ahead. Together, they would find a way to overcome the dark side of the GCN and realize the full potential of the Networked Mind.

A Glimmer of Hope

The research facility was bathed in the soft glow of the early morning light as Dr. Emily Carter sat in her office, surrounded by the remnants of a long and grueling night. The team had successfully defended against the hacker attack, but the toll it had taken was evident in the tired faces and weary eyes of her colleagues. Despite the exhaustion, there was a palpable sense of relief and cautious optimism in the air.

Emily leaned back in her chair, her eyes scanning the room. Reports and data sheets were scattered across her desk, each one a testament to the challenges they had faced and overcome. She took a deep breath, feeling a mix of pride and determination. They had managed to protect the Global Consciousness Network, but the journey was far from over.

Mark Thompson entered the office, carrying two steaming cups of coffee. He handed one to Emily, his expression a mix of fatigue and hope. "Morning, Emily. How are you holding up?"

Emily smiled, grateful for the gesture. "Thanks, Mark. I'm hanging in there. How's the team?"

"Exhausted but resilient," Mark replied, taking a seat across from her. "We've been through a lot, but I think we're stronger for it."

Emily nodded, her mind racing with the events of the past few days. "We need to assess the damage and plan our next steps. The hackers may have been thwarted for now, but we can't let our guard down."

Mark took a sip of his coffee, his eyes thoughtful. "Agreed. But I think we also need to take a moment to acknowledge what we've accomplished. We've faced some serious challenges, and we've come out the other side. That's no small feat."

Emily felt a surge of gratitude for Mark's unwavering support. "You're right. We need to celebrate our victories, even as we prepare for the next battle."

As they reviewed the data and discussed their plans, a knock on the door interrupted their conversation. Dr. James Lee, head of the cybersecurity team, entered the office, his face lit with a rare smile.

"Emily, Mark, I think we've found something," James said, holding up a tablet. "While analyzing the data from the attack, we discovered a potential breakthrough in enhancing the security and functionality of the GCN."

Emily's eyes widened with interest. "What did you find, James?"

James placed the tablet on the desk, displaying a series of graphs and diagrams. "The hackers' methods inadvertently revealed a way to strengthen our encryption protocols and improve the overall resilience of the network. It's a silver lining in an otherwise challenging situation."

Emily and Mark leaned in, studying the data. Emily felt a spark of hope ignite within her. "This is incredible, James. If we can implement these improvements, it could significantly enhance the security of the GCN and prevent future attacks."

Mark nodded, his expression brightening. "This could be the breakthrough we've been looking for. Let's get the team together and start working on this immediately."

As they gathered the research team and shared the news, the atmosphere in the room shifted from one of exhaustion to one of renewed energy and determination. The team members, despite their fatigue, were eager to dive into the new challenge and make the necessary improvements.

Emily felt a deep sense of pride as she watched her team work together, their dedication and resilience shining through. They had faced adversity and emerged stronger, ready to tackle whatever came next.

Later that day, as the team continued their work, Emily took a moment to reflect on the journey so far. The challenges they had faced had been daunting, but they had also revealed the strength and potential of the GCN. The vision of a connected world, where empathy and understanding transcended barriers, was within reach.

Mark approached her, his eyes filled with a mix of exhaustion and hope. "Emily, we've got a long road ahead, but I believe in what we're doing. The GCN has the potential to change the world, and we're making it happen."

Emily smiled, feeling a renewed sense of purpose. "Thank you, Mark. I couldn't do this without you and the team. Together, we'll overcome these challenges and realize the full potential of the Networked Mind."

In the quiet of the research facility, surrounded by the tools of their groundbreaking work, Emily felt a deep sense of resolve. The journey was far from over, but with the support of her team and the commitment to ethical development, she was ready to lead the way. Together, they would make the vision of the Networked Mind a reality.

8
CHAPTER 7: GLOBAL CRISIS

The Initial Outbreak

The research facility was unusually quiet, the air thick with an unspoken tension. Dr. Emily Carter and Dr. Mark Thompson stood in the main conference room, surrounded by their team. The large screen on the wall flickered to life, displaying a global news broadcast. The anchor's voice was grave, the words sending chills down Emily's spine.

"This just in: a massive breach in the Global Consciousness Network has caused widespread panic and chaos across multiple countries. Reports are coming in of severe mental overload, emotional distress, and even instances of violence as the network's vulnerabilities have been exploited on an unprecedented scale."

Emily's heart sank as she watched the footage of people in distress, their faces contorted with fear and confusion. The GCN, her creation, was at the center of a global crisis. She felt a wave of guilt and responsibility wash over her.

"Emily, we need to act fast," Mark said, his voice urgent. "We have to assess the situation and develop a plan to mitigate the damage."

Emily nodded, her mind racing. "Everyone, gather around. We need to understand the scope of this crisis and coordinate our response."

The team quickly assembled around the conference table, their faces etched with concern. Emily took a deep breath and began to speak. "We've been hit hard. The GCN's vulnerabilities have been exploited on a massive scale, and the impact is global. We need to work together to contain this and find a solution."

Dr. James Lee, head of the cybersecurity team, spoke up. "We've identified multiple entry points that the hackers used to breach the network. They're exploiting weaknesses we didn't even know existed. We need to shut them down immediately."

Dr. Sarah Mitchell, the neuroscientist, added, "The psychological impact on users is severe. We're seeing cases of mental overload and emotional distress. We need to provide support and resources to help them cope."

Emily felt the weight of the situation pressing down on her. "James, focus on securing the network and shutting down the entry points. Sarah, coordinate with mental health professionals to provide support for the affected users. Mark, we need to communicate with global authorities and coordinate our response."

Mark nodded, already reaching for his phone. "I'll start making calls. We need to get everyone on the same page."

As the team dispersed to tackle their respective tasks, Emily turned back to the screen, watching the news coverage with a heavy heart. The images of chaos and panic were a stark reminder of the responsibility she bore. She had envisioned the GCN as a tool for empathy and connection, but now it was causing harm on a global scale.

"Emily, we need to stay focused," Mark said, placing a reassuring hand on her shoulder. "We'll get through this. We just need to take it one step at a time."

Emily nodded, drawing strength from his words. "You're right. Let's get to work."

The hours that followed were a blur of activity. Emily and her team worked tirelessly, coordinating with governments and organizations around the world. They held emergency meetings, analyzed data, and developed strategies to contain the crisis.

"Emily, we've managed to shut down several of the entry points," James reported, his voice filled with determination. "But the hackers are persistent. We need to stay vigilant."

"Good work, James," Emily replied. "Keep me updated on your progress. We need to stay one step ahead."

As the day turned into night, the team continued their efforts, driven by a shared sense of urgency and purpose. Emily felt a mix of exhaustion and resolve. They were facing an unprecedented challenge, but she was determined to see it through.

"Emily, we've got a call with the UN in ten minutes," Mark said, his voice steady. "They're looking to us for guidance on how to handle the situation."

Emily took a deep breath, steeling herself for the conversation. "Let's do it. We need to show them that we're in control and that we have a plan."

As they prepared for the call, Emily felt a renewed sense of determination. The journey was far from over, but with the support of her team and the commitment to ethical development, she was ready to face whatever challenges lay ahead. Together, they would find a way to overcome the global crisis and realize the full potential of the Networked Mind.

Political and Social Turmoil

The atmosphere in the government office was tense as Dr. Emily Carter and Dr. Mark Thompson entered the meeting room. They were greeted by a group of stern-faced officials, their expressions a mix of concern and urgency. The global crisis sparked by the exploitation of the Global Consciousness Network had reached a critical point, and the world was looking to Emily and her team for answers.

"Thank you for coming, Dr. Carter, Dr. Thompson," said Secretary Jameson, a senior government official. "We need to understand the full scope of this crisis and what steps you're taking to address it."

Emily nodded, her heart heavy with the weight of responsibility. "Thank you for having us, Secretary Jameson. The situation is dire, but we're working around the clock to secure the GCN and provide support to those affected."

Mark stepped forward, his voice steady and authoritative. "We've identified the vulnerabilities that were exploited and are implementing measures to shut down the entry points. We're also coordinating with mental health professionals to support users experiencing distress."

The room was filled with murmurs as the officials absorbed their words. Emily could see the fear and skepticism in their eyes. She knew that rebuilding trust would be a monumental task.

"Dr. Carter, the public is demanding answers," said Senator Williams, his tone sharp. "People are scared, and they want to know how this happened and what you're doing to fix it."

Emily took a deep breath, her resolve strengthening. "We understand the public's concerns, Senator. The GCN was designed to foster empathy and connection, but its vulnerabilities have been exploited in ways we couldn't have anticipated. We're taking immediate action to secure the network and prevent further breaches. Transparency and accountability are our top priorities."

Another official, a representative from the Department of Homeland Security, spoke up. "What about the long-term implications? How can we ensure that the GCN won't be used as a tool for manipulation or control?"

Mark addressed the question with confidence. "We're establishing an independent oversight committee to monitor the GCN and ensure ethical standards are upheld. This committee will include representatives from various sectors, including ethics, law, and human rights. Our goal is to create a framework that prioritizes the safety and well-being of all users."

The discussion continued, with Emily and Mark fielding questions and providing detailed explanations of their plans. The officials were demanding but also seemed to appreciate the transparency and proactive approach.

As the meeting drew to a close, Secretary Jameson leaned forward, his expression serious. "Dr. Carter, Dr. Thompson, we need to see results. The world is watching, and we cannot afford any more failures."

Emily nodded, her determination unwavering. "We understand, Secretary Jameson. We're committed to resolving this crisis and ensuring the GCN is safe and beneficial for everyone."

After the meeting, Emily and Mark stepped outside into the bustling city streets. The air was filled with the sounds of traffic and the distant hum of conversations. They could see the tension and uncertainty in the faces of the people around them.

"Emily, we need to address the public directly," Mark said, his voice filled with urgency. "We need to show them that we're in control and that we're taking decisive action."

Emily agreed, her mind racing with the challenges ahead. "Let's hold a town hall meeting. We need to listen to their concerns and provide clear, honest answers."

The town hall meeting was held in a large auditorium, filled to capacity with concerned citizens, activists, and members of the media. Emily and Mark stood at the front, ready to face the crowd.

"Thank you all for coming," Emily began, her voice steady but compassionate. "We understand that you're scared and angry. The recent events have shaken us all, but we're here to listen and to work together to find solutions."

A woman in the front row stood up, her voice trembling with emotion. "My son has been using the GCN, and he's been experiencing severe anxiety and emotional distress. What are you doing to help people like him?"

Emily's heart ached at the woman's words. "I'm so sorry to hear that. We're providing resources and support to help those affected. We've partnered with mental health professionals to offer counseling and guidance. Your son's well-being is our top priority."

Another person, a young man with a determined expression, spoke up. "How can we trust that the GCN won't be used against us? What guarantees do we have?"

Mark addressed the question with confidence. "We're implementing enhanced security measures and establishing an independent oversight committee to ensure the GCN is used ethically and responsibly. Transparency and accountability are key, and we will keep you informed every step of the way."

The town hall continued, with Emily and Mark addressing a range of questions and concerns.

They knew that rebuilding trust would take time and consistent effort, but they were determined to show their commitment to making the GCN safe and beneficial for everyone.

As the meeting concluded, Emily felt a mix of exhaustion and determination. They had faced the public, acknowledged the challenges, and outlined their plan to address them. It was a crucial step forward, but the journey was far from over.

In the quiet of her office, surrounded by the tools of their groundbreaking work, Emily felt a deep sense of resolve. The journey was far from over, but with the support of her team and the commitment to ethical development, she was ready to face whatever challenges lay ahead. Together, they would find a way to overcome the global crisis and realize the full potential of the Networked Mind.

Personal Relationships Tested

The evening was quiet, the soft glow of the fireplace casting flickering shadows across the living room. Dr. Emily Carter sat on the couch, her mind heavy with the weight of the global crisis. The events of the past few days had taken a toll on her, and she felt the strain in every fiber of her being. She sipped her tea, trying to find a moment of peace amidst the chaos.

A knock on the door broke the silence. Emily set her cup down and went to answer it, finding her brother Alex standing on the doorstep. His expression was a mix of concern and determination.

"Alex, what are you doing here?" Emily asked, surprised but relieved to see him.

"I heard about the crisis," Alex replied, stepping inside. "I thought you might need someone to talk to."

Emily closed the door behind him and led him to the living room. They sat down, the fire providing a comforting warmth. For a moment, they sat in silence, the unspoken tension between them palpable.

"How have you been?" Emily finally asked, breaking the silence.

Alex shrugged. "I've been okay. Busy with work. But I've been following the news about the GCN. It sounds like you're facing some serious challenges."

Emily sighed, her shoulders slumping. "You have no idea. The negative side effects, the public backlash... It's all becoming overwhelming. I feel like I'm failing."

Alex looked at her, his eyes filled with empathy. "You're not failing, Emily. You're dealing with something incredibly complex. But you need to remember why you started this project in the first place."

Emily felt a lump form in her throat. "I wanted to create something that would bring people closer together, help them understand each other. But now it feels like it's causing more harm than good."

Alex reached out and took her hand, his touch grounding her. "Every innovation comes with challenges. The important thing is how you respond to them. You have the power to make things right."

Emily looked at her brother, seeing the sincerity in his eyes. "I just don't know if I can handle it all. The responsibility, the guilt... It's too much."

Alex squeezed her hand. "You don't have to do it alone. You have a team, and you have people who believe in you. And you have me, even if we haven't always seen eye to eye."

Emily felt tears welling up in her eyes. "Thank you, Alex. I needed to hear that."

They sat in silence for a while, the fire crackling softly. Emily felt a sense of relief, knowing that she wasn't alone in this struggle. She had her brother's support, and that meant more than she could express.

"Do you remember when we were kids, and we used to build those elaborate Lego structures?" Alex asked, a hint of a smile on his lips.

Emily chuckled, wiping away a tear. "Yeah, we always tried to outdo each other. But we also worked together to make something amazing."

Alex nodded. "Exactly. You have that same spirit now. You can face these challenges and find a way to make the GCN work. Just take it one step at a time."

Emily felt a renewed sense of determination. "You're right. I can't let the setbacks define the project. I need to focus on finding solutions and making things right."

Alex smiled, his eyes filled with pride. "That's the Emily I know. You're stronger than you think."

As the night wore on, they talked about their childhood, their dreams, and the challenges they had faced. Emily felt a sense of healing, the old wounds between them beginning to mend. She knew that the road ahead would be difficult, but she also knew that she had the strength and support to navigate it.

When Alex finally left, Emily felt a renewed sense of purpose. She returned to her desk, her mind clear and focused. She began drafting a plan to address the issues with the GCN, determined to make things right.

In the quiet of her home, surrounded by the warmth of the fire and the memories of her conversation with Alex, Emily felt a deep sense of resolve. The journey was far from over, but she was ready to face whatever challenges lay ahead. With the support of her team and the commitment to ethical development, she would find a way to overcome the unintended consequences and realize the full potential of the Networked Mind.

The Search for Solutions

The research facility was a hive of activity as Dr. Emily Carter and Dr. Mark Thompson led their team in a relentless search for solutions to the global crisis. The recent hacker attack had exposed critical vulnerabilities in the Global Consciousness Network, and the world was looking to them for answers. The stakes had never been higher.

Emily stood at the front of the main lab, surrounded by whiteboards covered in diagrams and equations. The air was thick with the scent of coffee and the hum of computers. Her team, a mix of neuroscientists, cybersecurity experts, and engineers, worked tirelessly at their stations, their faces etched with determination.

"Alright, everyone, let's review our progress," Emily said, her voice steady but urgent. "We've identified the key vulnerabilities that were exploited. Now we need to focus on securing those points and developing a comprehensive plan to prevent future breaches."

Dr. James Lee, head of the cybersecurity team, stepped forward. "We've enhanced our encryption protocols and deployed additional firewalls. But we need to go further. We should consider implementing a multi-layered security system that includes real-time monitoring and automated threat detection."

Emily nodded, her mind racing with possibilities. "That's a good start, James. We also need to improve user control. The tiered connection system is helping, but we need to provide more options for users to customize their experience and set boundaries."

Dr. Sarah Mitchell, the neuroscientist, added, "We should also focus on the psychological impact. Providing mental health resources and support groups is crucial, but we need to go beyond that. We need to develop tools that help users manage their emotional responses and prevent overload."

Mark, who had been coordinating with external experts, spoke up. "I've been in touch with several leading cybersecurity firms and mental health organizations. They're willing to collaborate with us and provide additional expertise. We need to bring them in and integrate their insights into our plan."

Emily felt a surge of gratitude for her team's dedication. "Thank you, Mark. Let's set up a series of brainstorming sessions with these experts. We need to explore every possible angle and leave no stone unturned."

As the team dispersed to tackle their respective tasks, Emily and Mark moved to a smaller meeting room to coordinate the next steps. The room was filled with charts and data sheets, a testament to the complexity of the challenge they faced.

"Emily, we need to keep morale high," Mark said, his voice filled with concern. "The team is exhausted, and the pressure is immense. We need to make sure they know how much we appreciate their hard work."

Emily nodded, her heart heavy with the weight of responsibility. "You're right, Mark. Let's organize a team meeting to acknowledge their efforts and provide some encouragement. We need to remind them that we're all in this together."

The team meeting was held later that afternoon. Emily stood at the front of the room, her eyes scanning the faces of her colleagues. She could see the fatigue and stress etched into their expressions, but she also saw the spark of determination that had carried them through the crisis.

"I want to thank each and every one of you for your incredible dedication and hard work," Emily began, her voice filled with emotion. "We've faced unprecedented challenges, but we've also made significant progress. Your efforts are making a difference, and I couldn't be prouder to work alongside you."

The room filled with murmurs of appreciation, and Emily felt a renewed sense of hope. "We have a long road ahead, but I believe in our ability to overcome these challenges. Together, we'll find a way to secure the GCN and ensure its potential to bring people closer together."

As the team returned to their work, Emily and Mark continued to coordinate the efforts, bringing in external experts and exploring innovative approaches. The brainstorming sessions were intense and productive, with ideas flowing freely and solutions taking shape.

"Emily, we've identified a new approach to enhance the security of the GCN," James reported during one of the sessions. "By integrating machine learning algorithms, we can create a system that adapts to new threats in real-time and provides continuous protection."

Emily's eyes lit up with excitement. "That's brilliant, James. Let's start working on the implementation. This could be a game-changer."

As the days turned into nights, the team worked tirelessly, driven by a shared sense of purpose and determination. Emily felt a deep sense of pride as she watched her colleagues collaborate and innovate, their resilience shining through.

In the quiet moments, Emily reflected on the journey so far. The challenges they had faced had been daunting, but they had also revealed the strength and potential of the GCN. The vision of a connected world, where empathy and understanding transcended barriers, was within reach.

Mark approached her, his eyes filled with a mix of exhaustion and hope. "Emily, we've got a long road ahead, but I believe in what we're doing. The GCN has the potential to change the world, and we're making it happen."

Emily smiled, feeling a renewed sense of purpose. "Thank you, Mark. I couldn't do this without you and the team. Together, we'll overcome these challenges and realize the full potential of the Networked Mind."

In the quiet of the research facility, surrounded by the tools of their groundbreaking work, Emily felt a deep sense of resolve. The journey was far from over, but with the support of her team and the commitment to ethical development, she was ready to lead the way. Together, they would make the vision of the Networked Mind a reality.

A Glimmer of Hope

The research facility was bathed in the soft glow of the early morning light as Dr. Emily Carter and Dr. Mark Thompson prepared for a global press conference. The past few days had been a whirlwind of intense work and sleepless nights, but the team had finally developed a plan to stabilize the Global Consciousness Network and address the crisis. The stakes were high, and the world was watching.

Emily stood in front of the mirror in her office, adjusting her blazer and taking a deep breath. She felt a mix of exhaustion and determination. This was their chance to show the world that they were in control and committed to making things right.

Mark knocked on the door, his expression serious but supportive. "Emily, it's time. Are you ready?"

Emily nodded, her resolve strengthening. "Let's do this."

They walked together to the press conference room, where a sea of reporters and cameras awaited them. The room buzzed with anticipation, the air thick with tension. Emily and Mark took their places at the podium, the bright lights casting harsh shadows on their faces.

"Good morning," Emily began, her voice steady but filled with emotion. "Thank you all for being here. Over the past few days, we have faced an unprecedented crisis. The Global Consciousness Network was exploited in ways we could not have anticipated, causing widespread panic and distress. We understand the gravity of the situation, and we are here to address your concerns and outline our plan to restore order."

The room fell silent, the reporters hanging on her every word. Emily glanced at Mark, who gave her a reassuring nod.

"We have been working around the clock to secure the GCN and provide support to those affected," Emily continued. "Our team has identified the key vulnerabilities that were exploited and has implemented measures to shut down the entry points. We have also enhanced our encryption protocols and deployed additional security measures to prevent future breaches."

Mark stepped forward to provide more details. "In addition to these technical measures, we are providing mental health resources and support to help users cope with the emotional impact of the crisis. We have partnered with leading mental health organizations to offer counseling and guidance. Our goal is to ensure the well-being of all users and restore trust in the GCN."

A reporter raised her hand, her expression serious. "Dr. Carter, how can you reassure the public that the GCN is safe and beneficial, given the recent events?"

Emily took a deep breath, her resolve unwavering. "We understand the public's concerns, and we are committed to addressing them. The GCN was created to foster empathy and understanding, and we believe in its potential to bring people closer together. We are taking every possible measure to ensure its safety and integrity. Transparency and accountability are key, and we will continue to keep the public informed about our progress and the steps we are taking to protect the GCN."

Another reporter asked, "What about the long-term implications? How can we ensure that the GCN won't be used as a tool for manipulation or control?"

Mark addressed the question with confidence. "We are establishing an independent oversight committee to monitor the GCN and ensure ethical standards are upheld. This committee will include representatives from various sectors, including ethics, law, and human rights. Our goal is to create a framework that prioritizes the safety and well-being of all users."

The press conference continued, with Emily and Mark addressing a range of questions and concerns. They knew that rebuilding public trust would take time and consistent effort, but they were determined to show their commitment to making the GCN safe and beneficial for everyone.

As the press conference drew to a close, Emily felt a mix of exhaustion and determination. They had faced the public, acknowledged the challenges, and outlined their plan to address them. It was a crucial step forward, but the journey was far from over.

Back in her office, Emily sat down at her desk, her mind racing with the events of the day. She knew that the road ahead would be difficult, but she was ready to face whatever challenges lay ahead. With the support of her team and the commitment to ethical development, she was determined to protect the GCN and realize its full potential.

Mark entered the office, his expression serious but hopeful. "You did great today, Emily. We made it clear that we're taking this seriously and that we're committed to finding solutions."

Emily smiled, feeling a renewed sense of purpose. "Thank you, Mark. We have a lot of work to do, but I believe in the vision of the GCN. Together, we'll find a way to overcome these challenges and create a better, more connected world."

In the quiet of her office, surrounded by the tools of their groundbreaking work, Emily felt a deep sense of resolve. The journey was far from over, but with the support of her team and the commitment to ethical development, she was ready to lead the way. Together, they would make the vision of the Networked Mind a reality.

9
CHAPTER 8: THE SEARCH FOR ANSWERS

Uncovering the Origins

The secure meeting room at the research facility was filled with a tense anticipation. Dr. Emily Carter and Dr. Mark Thompson stood at the head of the table, surrounded by their dedicated team. The recent crisis had shaken them all, but it had also ignited a fierce determination to uncover the truth behind the attacks on the Global Consciousness Network.

"Thank you all for coming," Emily began, her voice steady but urgent. "We've made significant progress in stabilizing the GCN, but we need to understand the origins of these attacks and the motivations behind them. Only then can we prevent future breaches."

The large screen at the front of the room displayed a series of data points and profiles. Emily clicked through the slides, highlighting key information. "We've identified several leads that could help us trace the origins of the hacker group. Our goal is to gather as much information as possible and piece together the full picture."

Dr. James Lee, head of the cybersecurity team, leaned forward. "We've analyzed the data from the recent attacks and found patterns that suggest a coordinated effort. These aren't random acts of sabotage; there's a clear strategy at play."

Dr. Sarah Mitchell, the neuroscientist, added, "We need to understand their motivations. Why are they targeting the GCN? What do they hope to achieve? Understanding their goals will help us anticipate their next moves."

Emily nodded, her mind racing with possibilities. "We've identified a few potential leads. There's a tech conference happening next week where several known hackers are expected to attend. We also have information about a hacker convention that could provide valuable insights."

Mark stepped in, his voice calm but determined. "We need to divide our efforts. Some of us will attend the tech conference, while others will go to the hacker convention. Our goal is to gather intel and make connections with potential informants."

The team members exchanged glances, their expressions a mix of determination and apprehension. Emily could sense the tension in the room. They were all aware of the risks involved, but they also knew that uncovering the truth was crucial.

Dr. Karen Foster, a psychologist on the team, voiced her concerns. "We need to be cautious. These environments can be unpredictable, and we don't want to draw unnecessary attention to ourselves. We should have a clear plan and contingency measures in place."

Emily appreciated Karen's caution. "You're right, Karen. We'll proceed carefully and ensure that we have backup plans. Our priority is to gather information without compromising our safety."

As the discussion continued, the team members debated the best approach to take. Some were eager to take bold actions and dive headfirst into the investigation, while others advocated for a more cautious and measured approach.

Dr. Lee spoke up again, his tone resolute. "We can't afford to be passive. The longer we wait, the more time the hackers have to plan their next move. We need to act decisively."

Emily felt the weight of the decision pressing down on her. She understood the urgency, but she also knew that they couldn't afford to make mistakes. "We'll strike a balance. We'll be proactive, but we'll also be careful. Let's finalize our plans and ensure that everyone is prepared."

The team spent the next few hours mapping out their strategy. They identified key individuals to approach, developed cover stories, and established communication protocols. Emily and Mark would lead the efforts at the tech conference, while Dr. Lee and Dr. Mitchell would head to the hacker convention.

As the meeting drew to a close, Emily addressed the team one last time. "This is a critical mission. We need to uncover the truth behind these attacks and protect the GCN. I have full confidence in each of you. Let's stay focused and work together."

The team members nodded, their expressions resolute. They knew the road ahead would be challenging, but they were ready to face whatever obstacles lay in their path.

In the quiet of the meeting room, surrounded by the tools of their groundbreaking work, Emily felt a renewed sense of determination. The journey was far from over, but with the support of her team and the commitment to uncovering the truth, she was ready to lead the way. Together, they would find the answers they sought and secure the future of the Networked Mind.

Following the Trail

The bustling atmosphere of the tech conference was a stark contrast to the tense, focused environment of the research facility. Dr. Emily Carter and Dr. Mark Thompson navigated through the crowded halls, their eyes scanning the sea of faces for any sign of potential informants. The conference was a hub of innovation and cutting-edge technology, but beneath the surface, it was also a gathering place for those who operated in the shadows.

"Keep your eyes open," Mark whispered, his voice barely audible over the din of conversations and presentations. "We need to find someone who can give us more information about the hacker group."

Emily nodded, her senses heightened. They had come prepared, armed with cover stories and a clear objective. Their goal was to make connections and gather intel without drawing too much attention to themselves.

As they moved through the conference, they spotted a familiar face—an independent cybersecurity expert named Alexei, known for his deep connections in the hacker community. Emily and Mark exchanged a glance, then approached him.

"Alexei, it's good to see you," Emily said, extending her hand. "I'm Emily Carter, and this is Mark

Thompson. We're here to learn more about the latest developments in cybersecurity."

Alexei shook her hand, his eyes narrowing slightly. "Emily Carter? The one behind the Global Consciousness Network? You've been making quite a splash lately."

Emily smiled, keeping her tone light. "Yes, that's me. We're always looking to improve and stay ahead of potential threats. We were hoping to pick your brain about some recent developments."

Alexei studied them for a moment, then nodded. "Alright, let's talk. There's a quiet spot over there."

They followed Alexei to a secluded corner of the conference hall, away from the prying eyes and ears of the crowd. Once they were seated, Alexei leaned in, his voice low.

"I've heard rumors about a group targeting the GCN," he said. "They're well-organized and have access to some serious resources. What do you know about them?"

Emily and Mark exchanged a glance. They had to tread carefully. "We've encountered some issues recently," Mark said, choosing his words carefully. "We're trying to understand their motivations and methods. Any information you can share would be invaluable."

Alexei nodded slowly. "They're not just hackers. They're ideologues. They believe the GCN is a tool for control and manipulation, and they're determined to expose its vulnerabilities. They're not in it for money or fame—they're on a mission."

Emily felt a chill run down her spine. "Do you know where we can find them? We need to understand their plans and stop them before they cause more harm."

Alexei hesitated, then glanced around to ensure they weren't being overheard. "There's a hacker convention happening in a few days. It's a bit more... underground. You'll find some of their members there. But be careful. These people are paranoid and dangerous."

Emily nodded, her mind racing. "Thank you, Alexei. We appreciate your help."

As they left the conference, Emily and Mark felt a renewed sense of urgency. They had a lead, but it was fraught with risks. The hacker convention would be a different environment, one where they would need to be even more cautious.

A few days later, they found themselves at the entrance of a dimly lit warehouse, the location of the hacker convention. The atmosphere was charged with a sense of secrecy and tension. Emily and Mark exchanged a glance, then stepped inside.

The convention was a maze of booths and makeshift stages, filled with people discussing everything from coding to cyber warfare. Emily and Mark moved through the crowd, their eyes scanning for potential informants.

They approached a booth where a group of hackers was demonstrating a new encryption-breaking tool. Emily struck up a conversation with one of them, a young woman with sharp eyes and a guarded demeanor.

"We're interested in learning more about the latest developments in cybersecurity," Emily said, keeping her tone casual. "We've heard about a group that's been making waves recently. Do you know anything about them?"

The woman studied them for a moment, then nodded. "You're talking about the ones targeting the GCN, right? They're serious. They believe they're fighting for a cause. But they're also very secretive. You won't find them easily."

Emily leaned in, her voice low. "We're not looking to cause trouble. We just want to understand their motivations. Can you point us in the right direction?"

The woman hesitated, then scribbled an address on a piece of paper. "This is where they usually meet. But be careful. They're not the trusting type."

Emily and Mark thanked her and left the convention, their minds racing with the new information. They had a location, but they knew the risks were high. They would need to be prepared for anything.

As they drove back to the research facility, Emily felt a mix of apprehension and determination. They were getting closer to uncovering the truth, but the journey was far from over. With the support of her team and the commitment to finding answers, she was ready to face whatever challenges lay ahead. Together, they would secure the future of the Networked Mind.

Hidden Agendas

The night was dark and cold as Dr. Emily Carter and Dr. Mark Thompson approached the remote location scribbled on the piece of paper they had received at the hacker convention. The address led them to an abandoned warehouse on the outskirts of the city, its windows boarded up and the surrounding area eerily quiet. Emily's heart pounded in her chest as they stepped out of the car, the weight of the unknown pressing down on her.

"Are you sure about this, Emily?" Mark asked, his voice low and cautious. "This could be a trap."

Emily nodded, her resolve unwavering. "We need to understand their motivations, Mark. This might be our only chance to get the information we need."

They approached the entrance, a heavy metal door that creaked ominously as they pushed it open. Inside, the warehouse was dimly lit, the air thick with the scent of dust and oil. They moved cautiously through the shadows, their footsteps echoing softly on the concrete floor.

"Stay close," Emily whispered, her eyes scanning the darkened space for any signs of movement.

As they ventured deeper into the warehouse, they spotted a group of figures huddled around a table, their faces illuminated by the glow of laptops and monitors. Emily and Mark exchanged a glance, then stepped forward, their presence immediately noticed by the group.

"Who are you?" one of the hackers demanded, his eyes narrowing with suspicion.

Emily raised her hands in a gesture of peace. "We're not here to cause trouble. We just want to talk."

The hacker studied them for a moment, then nodded to one of his companions. "Search them."

Two hackers approached, patting Emily and Mark down for weapons or recording devices. Satisfied that they were unarmed, the lead hacker gestured for them to sit.

"Alright, talk," he said, his tone guarded.

Emily took a deep breath, choosing her words carefully. "We're here to understand your motivations. We know you've been targeting the Global Consciousness Network, and we want to know why."

The hacker's eyes flashed with anger. "You want to know why? The GCN is a tool for control and manipulation. It's a threat to individual freedom and privacy. We're fighting to expose its dangers and bring it down."

Emily felt a chill run down her spine. "We created the GCN to foster empathy and understanding, not to control people. If there are issues, we want to address them. But we need to understand your perspective."

The hacker leaned back, his expression skeptical. "You really think you can fix it? The GCN is fundamentally flawed. It's too powerful, too invasive. People shouldn't have their thoughts and emotions connected like that."

Mark spoke up, his voice calm and measured. "We understand your concerns. But shutting down the GCN isn't the answer. We need to find a way to make it safe and beneficial for everyone."

The hacker's gaze softened slightly. "You really believe that, don't you? Maybe you're not like the others. But there are hidden agendas at play here. Powerful people who want to use the GCN for their own purposes."

Emily's heart raced. "What do you mean? Who are these people?"

The hacker hesitated, then glanced around to ensure they weren't being overheard. "There are corporations and government entities that see the GCN as a tool for surveillance and control. They're funding research and pushing for policies that would give them unprecedented access to people's minds."

Emily felt a surge of anger and determination. "We had no idea. We need to stop them. Will you help us?"

The hacker studied her for a moment, then nodded. "I'll give you what I know. But be careful. These people are powerful and dangerous."

As the hacker shared his information, Emily and Mark listened intently, their minds racing with the implications. They had uncovered a web of hidden agendas and powerful interests that threatened the very foundation of the GCN.

When the meeting concluded, Emily and Mark left the warehouse, their hearts heavy with the weight of the revelations. They had a new mission now—to expose the hidden agendas and protect the integrity of the GCN.

As they drove back to the research facility, Emily felt a renewed sense of purpose. The journey was far from over, but with the support of her team and the commitment to uncovering the truth, she was ready to face whatever challenges lay ahead. Together, they would secure the future of the Networked Mind and ensure that it remained a force for good.

Unexpected Allies

The research facility was abuzz with activity as Dr. Emily Carter and Dr. Mark Thompson returned from their clandestine meeting with the hacker group. The information they had gathered was both alarming and enlightening, revealing hidden agendas and powerful interests that threatened the integrity of the Global Consciousness Network. Emily knew they needed to act quickly to secure the GCN and prevent further exploitation.

As they entered the secure lab, the team looked up, their faces a mix of curiosity and concern. Emily and Mark gathered everyone around the large conference table, ready to share what they had learned.

"Thank you all for coming," Emily began, her voice steady but urgent. "We've uncovered some critical information about the hacker group and their motivations. There are powerful entities—corporations and government agencies—that see the GCN as a tool for surveillance and control. They're funding research and pushing for policies that would give them unprecedented access to people's minds."

The room fell silent as the team absorbed the gravity of the situation. Dr. James Lee, head of the cybersecurity team, was the first to speak. "This is worse than we thought. We need to act fast to secure the GCN and protect our users."

Dr. Sarah Mitchell, the neuroscientist, added, "We also need to address the psychological impact on users. If people find out about these hidden agendas, it could cause widespread panic and distrust."

Emily nodded, her mind racing with possibilities. "We need to develop a comprehensive plan to secure the GCN and ensure its ethical use. But we can't do this alone. We need allies—people who understand the stakes and are willing to help us."

Just as she finished speaking, the door to the lab opened, and a figure stepped inside. It was a young man with a determined expression and a hint of nervousness in his eyes. Emily recognized him immediately—it was the former hacker who had approached them at the convention.

"Hello, Dr. Carter, Dr. Thompson," he said, his voice steady but cautious. "My name is Ethan. I used to be part of the hacker group targeting the GCN. But I've seen the damage they're causing, and I want to help you secure the network."

The team exchanged glances, their expressions a mix of skepticism and curiosity. Emily stepped forward, her eyes fixed on Ethan. "Why should we trust you? How do we know you're not here to sabotage us?"

Ethan took a deep breath, his gaze unwavering. "I understand your skepticism. But I believe in the potential of the GCN to bring people together. I left the hacker group because I couldn't stand by and watch them destroy something that could do so much good. I have valuable information and skills that can help you secure the network."

Emily studied him for a moment, then nodded. "Alright, Ethan. We'll give you a chance. But you'll be under close supervision. We can't afford to take any risks."

Ethan nodded, his expression resolute. "I understand. I'll do whatever it takes to help."

As the team began to integrate Ethan into their efforts, trust issues inevitably arose. Some team members were wary of working with a former adversary, while others saw the potential benefits of his insider knowledge.

Dr. Karen Foster, the psychologist, voiced her concerns. "We need to be careful. Trust is fragile, and any misstep could jeopardize our efforts. We should establish clear guidelines and ensure that Ethan's contributions are closely monitored."

Emily agreed. "We'll set up a secure workspace for Ethan and assign a team member to work with him. We'll also conduct regular check-ins to ensure everything is on track."

Over the next few days, Ethan proved to be a valuable asset. His knowledge of the hacker group's methods and tactics allowed the team to anticipate and counter potential threats. He worked closely with Dr. Lee and the cybersecurity team, helping to develop new security protocols and enhance the GCN's defenses.

One evening, as the team gathered for a progress update, Ethan presented a breakthrough. "We've identified a way to strengthen the encryption protocols and create a multi-layered security system that adapts to new threats in real-time. This will significantly enhance the resilience of the GCN."

Emily felt a surge of hope. "That's incredible, Ethan. Let's start working on the implementation immediately."

As the team continued their efforts, Emily felt a renewed sense of purpose. They were making progress, and the collaboration with Ethan was proving to be a turning point. The journey was far from over, but with the support of her team and the commitment to ethical development, she was ready to face whatever challenges lay ahead.

In the quiet of the research facility, surrounded by the tools of their groundbreaking work, Emily felt a deep sense of resolve. Together, they would secure the future of the Networked Mind and ensure that it remained a force for good.

The True Extent Revealed

The research facility's large conference room was filled with a mix of anticipation and tension. Dr. Emily Carter and Dr. Mark Thompson stood at the front, ready to present their findings to government officials, media representatives, and their own research team. The stakes were high, and the room buzzed with the low hum of whispered conversations and the clicking of cameras.

Emily took a deep breath, her heart pounding with a mix of nerves and determination. This was their moment to reveal the true extent of the hacker group's plans and the hidden agendas they had uncovered. She glanced at Mark, who gave her a reassuring nod.

"Good morning, everyone," Emily began, her voice steady but filled with emotion. "Thank you for being here. Over the past few weeks, we have faced unprecedented challenges with the Global Consciousness Network. Today, we are here to share our findings and outline our strategy to secure the GCN and prevent future attacks."

The large screen behind her flickered to life, displaying a series of data points, profiles, and diagrams. Emily clicked through the slides, highlighting key information. "We have identified the hacker group responsible for the recent attacks. They are well-organized and have access to significant resources. Their goal is to expose what they believe are the dangers of the GCN and to bring it down."

Mark stepped forward, his voice calm and authoritative. "But that's not all. Through our investigation, we have uncovered hidden agendas involving powerful entities—corporations and government agencies—that see the GCN as a tool for surveillance and control. These entities are funding research and pushing for policies that would give them unprecedented access to people's minds."

The room fell silent as the audience absorbed the gravity of the revelations. Emily could see the shock and concern in their eyes. She knew that rebuilding trust would be a monumental task.

"We understand the seriousness of these findings," Emily continued. "And we are taking immediate action to secure the GCN and ensure its ethical use. We have enhanced our encryption protocols, deployed additional security measures, and established a multi-layered security system that adapts to new threats in real-time."

Mark added, "We are also providing mental health resources and support to help users cope with the emotional impact of the crisis. We have partnered with leading mental health organizations to offer counseling and guidance. Our goal is to ensure the well-being of all users and restore trust in the GCN."

A government official raised his hand, his expression serious. "Dr. Carter, Dr. Thompson, how can we be sure that these measures will be effective? What guarantees do we have that the GCN won't be exploited again?"

Emily took a deep breath, her resolve unwavering. "We are establishing an independent oversight committee to monitor the GCN and ensure ethical standards are upheld. This committee will include representatives from various sectors, including ethics, law, and human rights. Transparency and accountability are key, and we will continue to keep the public informed about our progress and the steps we are taking to protect the GCN."

Another official asked, "What about the long-term implications? How can we ensure that the GCN remains a force for good and not a tool for manipulation?"

Mark addressed the question with confidence. "We are committed to continuous improvement and ethical development. We will work closely with the oversight committee and external experts to ensure that the GCN is used responsibly and for the benefit of all. Our focus is on fostering empathy and understanding, and we will do everything in our power to protect that vision."

The press conference continued, with Emily and Mark addressing a range of questions and concerns. They knew that rebuilding public trust would take time and consistent effort, but they were determined to show their commitment to making the GCN safe and beneficial for everyone.

As the press conference drew to a close, Emily felt a mix of exhaustion and determination. They had faced the public, acknowledged the challenges, and outlined their plan to address them. It was a crucial step forward, but the journey was far from over.

Back in her office, Emily sat down at her desk, her mind racing with the events of the day. She knew that the road ahead would be difficult, but she was ready to face whatever challenges lay ahead. With the support of her team and the commitment to ethical development, she was determined to protect the GCN and realize its full potential.

Mark entered the office, his expression serious but hopeful. "You did great today, Emily. We made it clear that we're taking this seriously and that we're committed to finding solutions."

Emily smiled, feeling a renewed sense of purpose. "Thank you, Mark. We have a lot of work to do, but I believe in the vision of the GCN. Together, we'll find a way to overcome these challenges and create a better, more connected world."

In the quiet of her office, surrounded by the tools of their groundbreaking work, Emily felt a deep sense of resolve. The journey was far from

over, but with the support of her team and the commitment to ethical development, she was ready to lead the way. Together, they would make the vision of the Networked Mind a reality.

10
CHAPTER 9: REDEMPTION

The Plan

The secure meeting room at the research facility was filled with a sense of urgency and determination. Dr. Emily Carter stood at the head of the table, surrounded by her dedicated team. The recent revelations about the hacker group's hidden agendas and the powerful entities seeking to exploit the Global Consciousness Network had galvanized them all. They were ready to devise a comprehensive plan to restore balance and security to the GCN.

"Thank you all for being here," Emily began, her voice steady but filled with emotion. "We've faced unprecedented challenges, but we've also made significant progress. Today, we need to finalize our plan to secure the GCN and ensure its ethical use."

The large screen behind her displayed a series of data points, diagrams, and strategic outlines. Emily clicked through the slides, highlighting key aspects of their plan. "Our approach will focus on three main areas: enhancing security measures, improving user control, and providing comprehensive mental health support."

Dr. James Lee, head of the cybersecurity team, leaned forward. "We've already implemented several new encryption protocols and firewalls, but we need to go further. We should consider integrating machine learning algorithms to create a system that adapts to new threats in real-time."

Emily nodded, her mind racing with possibilities. "That's a great idea, James. We'll also need to establish a multi-layered security system that includes real-time monitoring and automated threat detection."

Dr. Sarah Mitchell, the neuroscientist, added, "We need to address the psychological impact on users. The tiered connection system is helping, but we need to provide more tools for users to manage their emotional responses and prevent overload. We should also expand our mental health resources and support groups."

Mark Thompson, who had been coordinating with external experts, spoke up. "I've been in touch with several leading cybersecurity firms and mental health organizations. They're willing to collaborate with us and provide additional expertise. We need to bring them in and integrate their insights into our plan."

Emily felt a surge of gratitude for her team's dedication. "Thank you, Mark. Let's set up a series of brainstorming sessions with these experts. We need to explore every possible angle and leave no stone unturned."

As the discussion continued, the team members debated the best approach to take. Some were eager to implement bold solutions and dive headfirst into the plan, while others advocated for a more cautious and measured approach.

Dr. Karen Foster, the psychologist, voiced her concerns. "We need to be careful. Trust is fragile, and any misstep could jeopardize our efforts. We should establish clear guidelines and ensure that our actions are both effective and ethical."

Emily appreciated Karen's caution. "You're right, Karen. We'll proceed carefully and ensure that our plan is both comprehensive and ethical. Our priority is to protect the GCN and its users."

Ethan, the former hacker who had joined their efforts, spoke up. "I can help with the technical aspects and provide insights into the hacker group's methods. But we need to be prepared for resistance. They won't give up easily."

Emily nodded, her resolve strengthening. "Thank you, Ethan. Your insights will be invaluable. We'll need to stay vigilant and be ready to adapt to any challenges that arise."

The team spent the next few hours mapping out their strategy in detail. They identified key tasks, assigned responsibilities, and established timelines. Emily and Mark would oversee the overall implementation, while James and Sarah would lead the efforts in their respective areas.

As the meeting drew to a close, Emily addressed the team one last time. "This is a critical mission. We need to restore balance and security to the GCN and ensure its ethical use. I have full confidence in each of you. Let's stay focused and work together."

The team members nodded, their expressions resolute. They knew the road ahead would be challenging, but they were ready to face whatever obstacles lay in their path.

In the quiet of the meeting room, surrounded by the tools of their groundbreaking work, Emily felt a renewed sense of determination. The journey was far from over, but with the support of her team and the commitment to ethical development, she was ready to lead the way. Together, they would find a way to secure the future of the Networked Mind and ensure that it remained a force for good.

Implementation Begins

The research facility buzzed with renewed energy as Dr. Emily Carter and Dr. Mark Thompson led their team in the implementation of their comprehensive plan to restore balance and security to the Global Consciousness Network. The stakes were high, and every member of the team was acutely aware of the importance of their work.

Emily stood in the cybersecurity lab, surrounded by monitors displaying real-time data and complex algorithms. Dr. James Lee and his team were hard at work, integrating the new encryption protocols and setting up the multi-layered security system.

"How's it going, James?" Emily asked, her eyes scanning the screens.

James looked up, his expression focused but determined. "We're making good progress. The machine learning algorithms are being integrated, and the real-time monitoring system is almost ready. This should significantly enhance our ability to detect and respond to threats."

Emily nodded, feeling a surge of hope. "Great work. Keep me updated on any issues."

Meanwhile, in the user support center, Dr. Sarah Mitchell and her team were busy developing new tools to help users manage their emotional responses and prevent overload. They were also expanding the mental health resources and support groups available to users.

"Sarah, how are things coming along here?" Emily asked as she entered the room.

Sarah smiled, though her eyes showed signs of fatigue. "We're rolling out the new tools and resources. The feedback from users has been positive so far. We're also training additional counselors to provide support."

Emily felt a deep sense of gratitude for her team's dedication. "Thank you, Sarah. Your work is making a real difference."

As the implementation continued, the team encountered several technical issues and unexpected obstacles. In the cybersecurity lab, a sudden spike in network activity triggered an alert.

"Emily, we've detected unusual activity," James reported, his fingers flying over the keyboard. "It looks like a potential breach attempt."

Emily's heart raced. "Can you isolate it?"

"We're working on it," James replied, his voice tense. "But it's sophisticated. We need to stay on high alert."

Emily and Mark coordinated with the cybersecurity team, ensuring that all measures were in place to counter the threat. The room was filled with the hum of computers and the rapid clicking of keyboards as the team worked tirelessly to secure the network.

In the user support center, Sarah and her team faced their own challenges. Some users were struggling with the new tools and resources, and the counselors were overwhelmed with requests for support.

"Emily, we need more resources," Sarah said, her voice strained. "The demand is higher than we anticipated."

Emily placed a reassuring hand on her shoulder. "We'll get you the support you need. Let's bring in additional counselors and expand our training programs."

Despite the setbacks, the team remained focused and determined. Emily and Mark provided leadership and support, keeping morale high and ensuring that everyone stayed on track.

One evening, as the team gathered for a progress update, Ethan presented a breakthrough. "We've identified a way to enhance the real-time monitoring system," he said, his eyes bright with excitement. "By integrating advanced pattern recognition algorithms, we can detect and respond to threats even more quickly."

Emily felt a surge of hope. "That's incredible, Ethan. Let's start working on the implementation immediately."

As the days turned into nights, the team continued their efforts, driven by a shared sense of purpose and determination. Emily felt a deep sense of pride as she watched her colleagues collaborate and innovate, their resilience shining through.

In the quiet moments, Emily reflected on the journey so far. The challenges they had faced had been daunting, but they had also revealed the strength and potential of the GCN. The vision of a connected world, where empathy and understanding transcended barriers, was within reach.

Mark approached her, his eyes filled with a mix of exhaustion and hope. "Emily, we've got a long road ahead, but I believe in what we're doing. The GCN has the potential to change the world, and we're making it happen."

Emily smiled, feeling a renewed sense of purpose. "Thank you, Mark. I couldn't do this without you and the team. Together, we'll overcome these challenges and realize the full potential of the Networked Mind."

In the quiet of the research facility, surrounded by the tools of their groundbreaking work, Emily felt a deep sense of resolve. The journey was far from over, but with the support of her team and the commitment to ethical development, she was ready to lead the way. Together, they would make the vision of the Networked Mind a reality.

Climax – Confrontation with the Hacker Group

The research facility was on high alert. The cybersecurity lab buzzed with tension as Dr. Emily Carter, Dr. Mark Thompson, and their team prepared for what they knew would be a critical confrontation. The hacker group, desperate to derail their efforts, had launched a final, aggressive attack on the Global Consciousness Network. The stakes had never been higher.

Emily stood at the center of the lab, surrounded by monitors displaying real-time data and flashing alerts. The air was thick with the hum of computers and the rapid clicking of keyboards. Dr. James Lee and his cybersecurity team were working furiously to fend off the attack.

"Emily, they're hitting us hard," James said, his voice strained. "They're using a multi-pronged approach, targeting multiple entry points simultaneously. We need to stay on top of this."

Emily nodded, her mind racing. "Deploy all available countermeasures. We can't let them breach the core of the network."

Mark, standing beside her, was coordinating with the rest of the team. "Ethan, we need your insights. How are they managing to sustain such a coordinated attack?"

Ethan, the former hacker who had joined their efforts, was at his station, his fingers flying over the keyboard. "They're using a distributed network of bots to amplify their attack. We need to isolate and neutralize the command nodes controlling the bots."

Emily felt a surge of determination. "James, can you pinpoint the command nodes?"

"We're working on it," James replied, his eyes fixed on the screen. "But it's like playing whack-a-mole. Every time we shut one down, another pops up."

The intensity of the attack strained the team's resources and morale. Emily could see the exhaustion in their faces, but she also saw their unwavering resolve. They had come too far to let the hackers win now.

"Emily, we've identified a pattern," Ethan said, his voice urgent. "They're using a specific sequence to coordinate the bots. If we can disrupt that sequence, we can break their control."

Emily's heart raced. "Do it, Ethan. Disrupt the sequence and shut them down."

Ethan's fingers flew over the keyboard as he executed the countermeasure. The room was filled with a tense silence as they watched the monitors, waiting to see if it would work.

Suddenly, the alerts began to subside. The relentless barrage of attacks slowed, then stopped altogether. The team let out a collective sigh of relief.

"We did it," James said, his voice filled with a mix of exhaustion and triumph. "We've neutralized their attack."

Emily felt a wave of relief wash over her. "Great work, everyone. But we can't let our guard down. They might try again."

As the team continued to monitor the network, Emily and Mark took a moment to reflect on the intensity of the confrontation. They had faced a formidable adversary, but their resilience and teamwork had carried them through.

"Ethan, your insights were invaluable," Mark said, placing a hand on Ethan's shoulder. "We couldn't have done this without you."

Ethan nodded, his expression a mix of relief and determination. "I'm just glad I could help. We need to stay vigilant. They won't give up easily."

Emily felt a deep sense of gratitude for her team's dedication. "Thank you, Ethan. And thank you, everyone. We've faced incredible challenges, but we've proven that we can overcome them together."

As the immediate threat subsided, the team took a moment to regroup and assess the situation. They had successfully defended against the hacker attack, but they knew that the journey was far from over.

In the quiet of the cybersecurity lab, surrounded by the tools of their groundbreaking work, Emily felt a renewed sense of resolve. The journey was far from over, but with the support of her team and the commitment to ethical development, she was ready to lead the way. Together, they would secure the future of the Networked Mind and ensure that it remained a force for good.

Aftermath and Reflection

The research facility was unusually quiet, the hum of the equipment a comforting backdrop as Dr. Emily Carter and Dr. Mark Thompson gathered their team in a small, quiet meeting room. The recent confrontation with the hacker group had been intense, but they had successfully defended the Global Consciousness Network. Now, it was time to reflect on their journey and the challenges they had overcome.

Emily stood at the head of the table, her eyes scanning the faces of her dedicated team. She could see the exhaustion etched into their expressions, but she also saw the spark of determination that had carried them through the crisis.

"Thank you all for being here," Emily began, her voice steady but filled with emotion. "We've faced incredible challenges over the past few weeks, but we've also made significant progress. I wanted to take a moment to reflect on what we've accomplished and discuss the impact of our work."

Dr. James Lee, head of the cybersecurity team, leaned forward. "We've enhanced the security of the GCN and implemented a multi-layered system that adapts to new threats in real-time. The recent attack was a testament to our resilience and our ability to protect the network."

Dr. Sarah Mitchell, the neuroscientist, added, "We've also expanded our mental health resources and support groups, providing users with the tools they need to manage their emotional responses. The feedback from users has been overwhelmingly positive."

Ethan, the former hacker who had joined their efforts, spoke up. "We've made great strides in securing the GCN, but we need to stay vigilant. The hacker group won't give up easily, and we need to be prepared for future challenges."

Emily nodded, her mind racing with the implications of their work. "You're right, Ethan. We need to stay focused and continue to improve the GCN. But I also want to acknowledge the personal sacrifices each of you has made. Your dedication and resilience have been truly inspiring."

Mark, who had been coordinating with external experts, spoke up. "We've also built strong partnerships with leading cybersecurity firms and mental health organizations. Their expertise has been invaluable, and we need to continue to collaborate with them to ensure the GCN remains a force for good."

The room fell silent as the team absorbed the gravity of their journey. Despite their victory, doubts and fears lingered. Emily could see the uncertainty in their eyes, and she knew she needed to inspire them to continue their work.

"Everyone, I know this has been a difficult journey," Emily said, her voice filled with conviction. "But we've proven that we can overcome incredible challenges. The GCN has the potential to change the world, and we are the ones who will make that happen. We need to believe in our vision and stay committed to our mission."

Dr. Karen Foster, the psychologist, nodded in agreement. "We've learned valuable lessons along the way. We've seen the importance of ethical development and the need to prioritize the well-being of our users. These principles will guide us as we move forward."

Emily felt a deep sense of pride as she looked around the room. "Thank you, Karen. And thank you, everyone. Your hard work and dedication have brought us to this point. Let's continue to work together and make the GCN a tool for empathy, understanding, and connection."

As the meeting drew to a close, the team members exchanged words of encouragement and support. They knew the road ahead would be challenging, but they were ready to face whatever obstacles lay in their path.

In the quiet of the meeting room, surrounded by the tools of their groundbreaking work, Emily felt a renewed sense of resolve. The journey was far from over, but with the support of her team and the commitment to ethical development, she was ready to lead the way. Together, they would secure the future of the Networked Mind and ensure that it remained a force for good.

A New Beginning

The research facility was filled with a sense of anticipation as Dr. Emily Carter and Dr. Mark Thompson prepared for the global press conference. The past few weeks had been a whirlwind of intense work and sleepless nights, but the team had successfully implemented their plan to restore balance and security to the Global Consciousness Network. Today, they would share their progress with the world.

Emily stood in front of the mirror in her office, adjusting her blazer and taking a deep breath. She felt a mix of exhaustion and determination. This was their moment to show the world that they were in control and committed to making things right.

Mark knocked on the door, his expression serious but supportive. "Emily, it's time. Are you ready?"

Emily nodded, her resolve strengthening. "Let's do this."

They walked together to the press conference room, where a sea of reporters and cameras awaited them. The room buzzed with anticipation, the air thick with tension. Emily and Mark took their places at the podium, the bright lights casting harsh shadows on their faces.

"Good morning," Emily began, her voice steady but filled with emotion. "Thank you all for being here. Over the past few weeks, we have faced unprecedented challenges with the Global Consciousness Network. Today, we are here to share our progress and outline the steps we have taken to secure the GCN and ensure its ethical use."

The large screen behind her flickered to life, displaying a series of data points, diagrams, and strategic outlines. Emily clicked through the slides, highlighting key aspects of their plan. "Our approach has focused on three main areas: enhancing security measures, improving user control, and providing comprehensive mental health support."

Mark stepped forward, his voice calm and authoritative. "We have implemented new encryption protocols and established a multi-layered security system that adapts to new threats in real-time. We have also expanded our mental health resources and support groups, providing users with the tools they need to manage their emotional responses and prevent overload."

A reporter raised her hand, her expression serious. "Dr. Carter, how can you reassure the public that the GCN is safe and beneficial, given the recent events?"

Emily took a deep breath, her resolve unwavering. "We understand the public's concerns, and we are committed to addressing them. The GCN was created to foster empathy and understanding, and we believe in its potential to bring people closer together. We are taking every possible measure to ensure its safety and integrity. Transparency and accountability are key, and we will continue to keep the public informed about our progress and the steps we are taking to protect the GCN."

Another reporter asked, "What about the long-term implications? How can we ensure that the GCN remains a force for good and not a tool for manipulation?"

Mark addressed the question with confidence. "We are establishing an independent oversight committee to monitor the GCN and ensure ethical standards are upheld. This committee will include representatives from various sectors, including ethics, law, and human rights. Our goal is to create a framework that prioritizes the safety and well-being of all users."

The press conference continued, with Emily and Mark addressing a range of questions and concerns. They knew that rebuilding public trust would take time and consistent effort, but they were determined to show their commitment to making the GCN safe and beneficial for everyone.

As the press conference drew to a close, Emily felt a mix of exhaustion and determination. They had faced the public, acknowledged the challenges, and outlined their plan to address them. It was a crucial step forward, but the journey was far from over.

Back in her office, Emily sat down at her desk, her mind racing with the events of the day. She knew that the road ahead would be difficult, but she was ready to face whatever challenges lay ahead. With the support of her team and the commitment to ethical development, she was determined to protect the GCN and realize its full potential.

Mark entered the office, his expression serious but hopeful. "You did great today, Emily. We made it clear that we're taking this seriously and that we're committed to finding solutions."

Emily smiled, feeling a renewed sense of purpose. "Thank you, Mark. We have a lot of work to do, but I believe in the vision of the GCN. Together, we'll find a way to overcome these challenges and create a better, more connected world."

In the quiet of her office, surrounded by the tools of their groundbreaking work, Emily felt a deep sense of resolve. The journey was far from over, but with the support of her team and the commitment to ethical development, she was ready to lead the way. Together, they would make the vision of the Networked Mind a reality.

11

CHAPTER 10: NEW BEGINNINGS

The Aftermath

The research facility was alive with a quiet hum of activity as Dr. Emily Carter walked through the various labs and offices. The air was filled with a sense of accomplishment and relief. The team had successfully implemented their plan to restore balance and security to the Global Consciousness Network, and the positive feedback from users was pouring in.

Emily entered the main lab, where Dr. James Lee and his cybersecurity team were gathered around a cluster of monitors. The screens displayed real-time data, showing the stability and security of the GCN. James looked up as Emily approached, a satisfied smile on his face.

"Emily, the new security measures are holding strong," James reported. "We've seen a significant decrease in attempted breaches, and the real-time monitoring system is working flawlessly."

Emily felt a surge of pride. "That's fantastic news, James. Your team's hard work is paying off."

She continued her walk through the facility, stopping by the user support center where Dr. Sarah Mitchell and her team were busy assisting users. The atmosphere was one of calm efficiency, a stark contrast to the chaos of the past few weeks.

"Sarah, how are things going here?" Emily asked.

Sarah smiled, though her eyes showed signs of fatigue. "We've had a lot of positive feedback from users. The new tools and resources are helping them manage their emotional responses, and the support groups are making a real difference."

Emily felt a deep sense of gratitude for her team's dedication. "Thank you, Sarah. Your work is making a real impact."

As she moved through the facility, Emily took a moment to reflect on the journey they had been on. The challenges had been immense, but the team's resilience and determination had carried them through. They had faced down a formidable adversary and emerged stronger for it.

In the main conference room, Emily found Mark Thompson reviewing a series of reports. He looked up as she entered, his expression one of satisfaction and relief.

"Emily, the feedback from users and partners has been overwhelmingly positive," Mark said. "We've received messages of support and gratitude from all over the world."

Emily smiled, feeling a sense of accomplishment. "That's wonderful to hear, Mark. We've come a long way."

They gathered the team for a brief meeting to acknowledge their hard work and dedication. Emily stood at the head of the table, her eyes scanning the faces of her colleagues. She could see the exhaustion etched into their expressions, but she also saw the spark of determination that had carried them through the crisis.

"Thank you all for being here," Emily began, her voice steady but filled with emotion. "We've faced incredible challenges over the past few weeks, but we've also made significant progress. I wanted to take a moment to acknowledge your hard work and dedication. Your efforts have made a real difference, and I couldn't be prouder to work alongside you."

The room filled with murmurs of appreciation, and Emily felt a renewed sense of hope. "We've restored balance and security to the GCN, but our work is far from over. We need to stay vigilant and continue to improve the network to ensure its long-term stability and security."

Dr. Karen Foster, the psychologist, nodded in agreement. "We've learned valuable lessons along the way. We've seen the importance of ethical development and the need to prioritize the well-being of our users. These principles will guide us as we move forward."

Emily felt a deep sense of pride as she looked around the room. "Thank you, Karen. And thank you, everyone. Your hard work and dedication have brought us to this point. Let's continue to work together and make the GCN a tool for empathy, understanding, and connection."

As the meeting drew to a close, the team members exchanged words of encouragement and support. They knew the road ahead would be challenging, but they were ready to face whatever obstacles lay in their path.

In the quiet of the research facility, surrounded by the tools of their groundbreaking work, Emily felt a renewed sense of resolve. The journey was far from over, but with the support of her team and the commitment to ethical development, she was ready to lead the way. Together, they would secure the future of the Networked Mind and ensure that it remained a force for good.

Rebuilding Trust

The town hall was packed, the air buzzing with a mix of anticipation and tension. Dr. Emily Carter and Dr. Mark Thompson stood at the front of the room, facing a diverse crowd of community members, activists, and curious onlookers. The recent crisis with the Global Consciousness Network had shaken public trust, and this meeting was a crucial step in rebuilding that trust and fostering open dialogue.

"Thank you all for coming," Emily began, her voice steady but warm. "We understand that the recent events have caused a lot of concern and fear. We're here to listen to your feedback, address your concerns, and share our vision for the future of the GCN."

The room was arranged with rows of chairs facing a stage, where Emily and Mark stood behind a podium. The large screen behind them displayed key points and data about the GCN's recent improvements and security measures.

A hand shot up from the middle of the crowd. "Dr. Carter, my name is Rachel, and I've been using the GCN in my therapy practice. It's been incredibly helpful for understanding my clients' emotions, but I'm concerned about the long-term effects. How do we ensure that this technology doesn't become a crutch?"

Emily nodded, appreciating the thoughtful question. "That's a valid concern, Rachel. The GCN is a tool to enhance communication and empathy, but it should not replace traditional methods of therapy and support. We encourage users to balance their use of the GCN with other forms of interaction and self-care. Ongoing research and feedback from professionals like you will help us develop guidelines to ensure its responsible use."

Another hand went up, this time from a young man in the back. "I'm a high school teacher, and I've noticed that some students are becoming overly reliant on the GCN for social interactions. They're struggling to communicate without it. How do we address this issue?"

Mark stepped forward to answer. "That's an important observation. The GCN is meant to complement, not replace, face-to-face interactions. We need to educate users, especially young people, about the importance of maintaining a balance. We're working on developing educational programs and resources to help integrate the GCN in a healthy and constructive way."

The discussion continued, with a range of opinions and experiences being shared. Some people praised the GCN for its ability to foster deeper connections and understanding, while others raised concerns about privacy, security, and the potential for misuse.

A middle-aged man named Tom stood up, his expression serious. "I've read reports about potential security breaches. How can we be sure that our thoughts and emotions are safe from hackers?"

Emily took a deep breath, ready to address the tough question. "Security is a top priority for us. Each connection within the GCN is encrypted, and we have implemented robust cybersecurity protocols to protect against unauthorized access. We're also working with leading experts in the field to continuously improve our defenses. Additionally, the independent oversight committee will monitor the network to ensure ethical standards are upheld."

The room buzzed with murmurs as people absorbed her words. Emily could see the mix of emotions on their faces—hope, fear, curiosity, and skepticism. She knew that building trust would take time and effort.

A young woman named Jessica raised her hand, her voice filled with emotion. "My brother has been using the GCN to connect with our family. It's helped him feel less isolated, but I'm worried about the emotional intensity. Sometimes it feels overwhelming."

Emily's heart ached at the genuine concern in Jessica's voice. "Thank you for sharing that, Jessica. We're aware of the potential for emotional overload, and we're working on ways to moderate the intensity of the connections. The tiered connection system allows users to gradually increase their level of engagement, helping them acclimate to the shared experiences. Your feedback is crucial in helping us refine these features."

As the feedback session continued, Emily and Mark listened intently, taking notes and addressing each concern with empathy and clarity. They knew that the success of the GCN depended on the trust and support of the public.

After the session, Emily and Mark returned to their office, exhausted but optimistic. They reviewed the feedback and discussed the next steps, focusing on refining the GCN and addressing the concerns raised.

"Emily, I think we made a real impact today," Mark said, his voice filled with determination. "People are starting to see the potential of the GCN, but we need to keep working hard to earn their trust."

Emily nodded, her mind racing with ideas. "Agreed. We'll take the feedback we've received and use it to improve the GCN. We're on the right path, but we need to keep pushing forward."

In the quiet of the research facility, surrounded by the tools of their groundbreaking work, Emily felt a renewed sense of purpose. The vision of a connected world was within reach, and with the support of their team and the commitment to ethical development, they were ready to face whatever challenges lay ahead. Together, they would make the vision of the Networked Mind a reality.

Expanding the Network

The research facility was abuzz with excitement as Dr. Emily Carter and Dr. Mark Thompson prepared for a global conference. The team had been working tirelessly to expand the Global Consciousness Network to new regions and demographics, ensuring that the technology was accessible and beneficial to a diverse range of users. Today, they would present their progress and share their vision for the future.

Emily stood in the main conference room, surrounded by her team. The large screen behind her displayed a world map, highlighting the regions where the GCN had been successfully implemented. She felt a surge of pride as she looked at the faces of her colleagues, each one reflecting the dedication and hard work that had brought them to this point.

"Thank you all for being here," Emily began, her voice steady but filled with excitement. "We've made incredible progress in expanding the GCN, and today, we'll be sharing our achievements with the world. This is a testament to your hard work and commitment to our vision."

Dr. James Lee, head of the cybersecurity team, nodded in agreement. "We've enhanced the security measures and ensured that the GCN is robust enough to handle the increased load. Our real-time monitoring system is working flawlessly, and we've received positive feedback from users in the new regions."

Dr. Sarah Mitchell, the neuroscientist, added, "We've also tailored our mental health resources to meet the needs of diverse populations. We've partnered with local organizations to provide culturally relevant support and ensure that users feel understood and supported."

Mark stepped forward, his expression one of satisfaction and determination. "We've built strong partnerships with international organizations and governments. Their support has been invaluable in helping us navigate the logistical and cultural challenges of expanding the GCN."

As the team continued to discuss their progress, Emily felt a deep sense of gratitude for their dedication. They had faced numerous obstacles, but their resilience and determination had carried them through.

Later that day, Emily and Mark stood on the stage at the global conference, facing an audience of international partners, media representatives, and curious onlookers. The room was filled with anticipation as they prepared to share their vision for the future of the GCN.

"Good morning, everyone," Emily began, her voice steady but filled with emotion. "Thank you for joining us today. Over the past few months, we have worked tirelessly to expand the Global Consciousness Network to new regions and demographics. Our goal is to create a more connected and empathetic world, and we are excited to share our progress with you."

The large screen behind her displayed a series of data points, maps, and testimonials from users around the world. Emily clicked through the slides, highlighting key achievements and milestones.

"We have successfully implemented the GCN in several new regions, including rural areas and underserved communities," Emily continued. "Our partnerships with local organizations have been crucial in ensuring that the technology is accessible and beneficial to a diverse range of users."

Mark stepped forward to provide more details. "We have also focused on enhancing the security and stability of the GCN. Our multi-layered security system and real-time monitoring capabilities have proven effective in protecting the network and ensuring a positive user experience."

A representative from an international organization raised her hand, her expression one of curiosity. "Dr. Carter, how have you addressed the cultural differences and unique needs of the new regions where the GCN has been implemented?"

Emily smiled, appreciating the thoughtful question. "We have worked closely with local partners to understand the cultural context and tailor our approach accordingly. This includes providing culturally relevant mental health resources and support, as well as ensuring that the technology is accessible and user-friendly for all populations."

Another attendee asked, "What are your plans for further expansion? How do you ensure that the GCN remains a force for good as it continues to grow?"

Mark addressed the question with confidence. "We are committed to continuous improvement and ethical development. Our independent oversight committee will monitor the GCN and ensure that it is used responsibly and for the benefit of all. We will also continue to build strong partnerships with international organizations and governments to support our expansion efforts."

The conference continued, with Emily and Mark addressing a range of questions and sharing their vision for the future. They knew that expanding the GCN would come with challenges, but they were determined to navigate them with empathy and transparency.

As the conference drew to a close, Emily felt a mix of exhaustion and determination. They had shared their progress and vision with the world, but the journey was far from over. With the support of their team and the commitment to ethical development, they were ready to face whatever challenges lay ahead.

In the quiet of the research facility, surrounded by the tools of their groundbreaking work, Emily felt a deep sense of resolve. The vision of a connected world was within reach, and with the support of their team and the commitment to ethical development, they were ready to lead the way. Together, they would make the vision of the Networked Mind a reality.

Personal Growth

The evening was calm and serene as Dr. Emily Carter returned home, the weight of the past few months finally beginning to lift. The challenges with the Global Consciousness Network had tested her in ways she had never imagined, but they had also brought about profound personal growth. Tonight, she had invited her brother Alex and a few close friends over for a quiet evening, a chance to reconnect and reflect on their journey.

The aroma of home-cooked food filled the air as Emily set the table, her mind drifting back to the countless hours spent at the research facility. The doorbell rang, pulling her from her thoughts.

She opened the door to find Alex standing there, a warm smile on his face.

"Hey, Em," Alex said, giving her a hug. "How are you holding up?"

Emily smiled, feeling a sense of comfort in his presence. "I'm doing better, Alex. It's been a tough few months, but we're making progress."

As they settled into the living room, Emily's close friends arrived, their faces lighting up with smiles and laughter. The atmosphere was relaxed and filled with a sense of camaraderie. They gathered around the table, sharing stories and reminiscing about old times.

"Emily, you've been through so much," said Lisa, one of her oldest friends. "How are you managing everything?"

Emily took a deep breath, her eyes reflecting the weight of her experiences. "It's been challenging, but I've learned a lot about myself and what I'm capable of. The support from all of you and my team has been invaluable."

Alex nodded, his expression thoughtful. "You've always been strong, Em. But it's important to take care of yourself too. You can't pour from an empty cup."

Emily smiled, appreciating his concern. "I know, Alex. I'm trying to find a balance. Tonight is a step in that direction."

As they enjoyed their meal, the conversation shifted to lighter topics, filled with laughter and shared memories. Emily felt a sense of warmth and connection, a reminder of the importance of her personal relationships amidst the pressures of her professional life.

Later in the evening, as the group moved to the living room, Alex and Emily found a quiet moment to talk. The fire crackled softly, casting a warm glow over the room.

"Em, I'm really proud of you," Alex said, his voice sincere. "You've faced incredible challenges and come out stronger. But remember, it's okay to lean on others when you need to."

Emily felt a lump form in her throat. "Thank you, Alex. Your support means more than you know. I've realized that I can't do everything alone, and that's okay."

They sat in comfortable silence for a moment, the bond between them stronger than ever. Emily felt a sense of peace, knowing that she had the support of her loved ones as she continued her journey.

As the evening drew to a close, Emily's friends began to leave, each one offering words of encouragement and support. Emily stood at the door, feeling a renewed sense of purpose and determination.

"Thank you all for being here," she said, her voice filled with gratitude. "Your support means the world to me."

Lisa hugged her tightly. "We're always here for you, Emily. Don't forget that."

As the last of her friends left, Emily and Alex sat by the fire, the warmth and light a comforting presence. Emily felt a deep sense of resolve, ready to face whatever challenges lay ahead.

"Alex, I know the road ahead won't be easy," Emily said, her voice steady. "But with the support of my team and the people I care about, I know we can make the GCN a force for good."

Alex smiled, his eyes filled with pride. "I believe in you, Em. And I know you'll make it happen."

In the quiet of her home, surrounded by the warmth of the fire and the love of her family and friends, Emily felt a renewed sense of hope. The journey was far from over, but she was ready to lead the way. Together, they would make the vision of the Networked Mind a reality.

Looking to the Future

The research facility was abuzz with anticipation as Dr. Emily Carter and Dr. Mark Thompson prepared for the global press conference. The past few months had been a whirlwind of intense work and sleepless nights, but the team had successfully implemented their plan to restore balance and security to the Global Consciousness Network. Today, they would share their vision for the future with the world.

Emily stood in front of the mirror in her office, adjusting her blazer and taking a deep breath. She felt a mix of exhaustion and determination. This was their moment to show the world that they were in control and committed to making things right.

Mark knocked on the door, his expression serious but supportive. "Emily, it's time. Are you ready?"

Emily nodded, her resolve strengthening. "Let's do this."

They walked together to the press conference room, where a sea of reporters and cameras awaited them. The room buzzed with anticipation, the air thick with tension. Emily and Mark took their places at the podium, the bright lights casting harsh shadows on their faces.

"Good morning," Emily began, her voice steady but filled with emotion. "Thank you all for being here. Over the past few months, we have faced unprecedented challenges with the Global Consciousness Network. Today, we are here to share our progress and outline our vision for the future."

The large screen behind her flickered to life, displaying a series of data points, diagrams, and strategic outlines. Emily clicked through the slides, highlighting key aspects of their plan. "Our approach has focused on three main areas: enhancing security measures, improving user control, and providing comprehensive mental health support."

Mark stepped forward, his voice calm and authoritative. "We have implemented new encryption protocols and established a multi-layered security system that adapts to new threats in realtime. We have also expanded our mental health resources and support groups, providing users with the tools they need to manage their emotional responses and prevent overload."

A reporter raised her hand, her expression serious. "Dr. Carter, how can you reassure the public that the GCN is safe and beneficial, given the recent events?"

Emily took a deep breath, her resolve unwavering. "We understand the public's concerns, and we are committed to addressing them. The GCN was created to foster empathy and understanding, and we believe in its potential to bring people closer together. We are taking every possible measure to ensure its safety and integrity. Transparency and accountability are key, and we will continue to keep the public informed about our progress and the steps we are taking to protect the GCN."

Another reporter asked, "What about the long-term implications? How can we ensure that the GCN remains a force for good and not a tool for manipulation?"

Mark addressed the question with confidence. "We are establishing an independent oversight committee to monitor the GCN and ensure ethical standards are upheld. This committee will include representatives from various sectors, including ethics, law, and human rights. Our goal is to create a framework that prioritizes the safety and well-being of all users."

The press conference continued, with Emily and Mark addressing a range of questions and concerns. They knew that rebuilding public trust would take time and consistent effort, but they were determined to show their commitment to making the GCN safe and beneficial for everyone.

As the press conference drew to a close, Emily felt a mix of exhaustion and determination. They had faced the public, acknowledged the challenges, and outlined their plan to address them. It was a crucial step forward, but the journey was far from over.

Back in her office, Emily sat down at her desk, her mind racing with the events of the day. She knew that the road ahead would be difficult, but she was ready to face whatever challenges lay ahead. With the support of her team and the commitment to ethical development, she was determined to protect the GCN and realize its full potential.

Mark entered the office, his expression serious but hopeful. "You did great today, Emily. We made it clear that we're taking this seriously and that we're committed to finding solutions."

Emily smiled, feeling a renewed sense of purpose. "Thank you, Mark. We have a lot of work to do, but I believe in the vision of the GCN. Together, we'll find a way to overcome these challenges and create a better, more connected world."

In the quiet of her office, surrounded by the tools of their groundbreaking work, Emily felt a deep sense of resolve. The journey was far from over, but with the support of her team and the commitment to ethical development, she was ready to lead the way. Together, they would make the vision of the Networked Mind a reality.

12
CHAPTER 11: THE NETWORK EXPANDS

Strategic Planning

The strategic planning meeting room at the research facility was filled with a sense of purpose and anticipation. Dr. Emily Carter stood at the head of the table, surrounded by her dedicated team and international partners. The large screen behind her displayed a world map, highlighting potential regions for the expansion of the Global Consciousness Network. Today, they would finalize their strategic plan to bring the GCN to new areas and demographics.

"Thank you all for being here," Emily began, her voice steady but filled with excitement. "We've made incredible progress in restoring balance and security to the GCN. Now, it's time to expand our reach and ensure that this technology is accessible and beneficial to a diverse range of users."

Dr. James Lee, head of the cybersecurity team, nodded in agreement. "We've identified several regions where the GCN could have a significant impact. These include rural areas, underserved communities, and regions with limited access to mental health resources."

Dr. Sarah Mitchell, the neuroscientist, added, "We need to tailor our approach to meet the specific needs of these populations. This includes providing culturally relevant support and ensuring that the technology is user-friendly for all demographics."

Mark Thompson, who had been coordinating with international partners, spoke up. "We've built strong relationships with local organizations and governments. Their support will be crucial in navigating the logistical and cultural challenges of expanding the GCN."

As the discussion continued, the team analyzed data, identified target areas, and developed a comprehensive approach to ensure the success of the expansion. Emily felt a deep sense of pride as she listened to her colleagues' insights and ideas.

"We need to ensure that our plan is both effective and inclusive," Emily said, her voice firm. "This means addressing logistical challenges, such as infrastructure and connectivity, as well as cultural considerations. We need to work closely with local leaders and community members to understand their needs and tailor our approach accordingly."

Dr. Karen Foster, the psychologist, voiced her concerns. "We also need to be mindful of potential resistance. Some communities may be wary of new technology, especially one that involves sharing thoughts and emotions. We need to build trust and demonstrate the benefits of the GCN."

Emily nodded, appreciating Karen's caution. "You're right, Karen. Trust is crucial. We need to engage with communities, listen to their concerns, and provide clear, transparent information about the GCN and its benefits."

As the team continued to brainstorm, differing opinions emerged about the best approach to take. Some members advocated for a bold, rapid expansion, while others favored a more cautious, incremental approach.

Dr. Lee spoke up, his tone resolute. "We can't afford to be passive. The sooner we implement the GCN in these regions, the sooner we can start making a positive impact."

Dr. Mitchell countered, "But we need to ensure that we're doing it right. Rushing the process could lead to mistakes and undermine our efforts. We need to be thorough and considerate."

Emily felt the weight of the decision pressing down on her. She understood the urgency, but she also knew that they couldn't afford to make mistakes. "We'll strike a balance. We'll be proactive, but we'll also be careful. Let's finalize our plans and ensure that everyone is prepared."

The team spent the next few hours mapping out their strategy in detail. They identified key tasks, assigned responsibilities, and established timelines. Emily and Mark would oversee the overall implementation, while James and Sarah would lead the efforts in their respective areas.

As the meeting drew to a close, Emily addressed the team one last time. "This is a critical mission. We need to ensure that the GCN is accessible and beneficial to all. I have full confidence in each of you. Let's stay focused and work together."

The team members nodded, their expressions resolute. They knew the road ahead would be challenging, but they were ready to face whatever obstacles lay in their path.

In the quiet of the meeting room, surrounded by the tools of their groundbreaking work, Emily felt a renewed sense of determination. The journey was far from over, but with the support of her team and the commitment to ethical development, she was ready to lead the way. Together, they would expand the reach of the Networked Mind and ensure that it remained a force for good.

Pilot Programs

The sun was just beginning to rise as Dr. Emily Carter and Dr. Mark Thompson arrived in a small rural village, one of the first locations selected for the pilot program of the Global Consciousness Network. The air was crisp, and the village was slowly coming to life, with people starting their day and children heading off to school. Emily felt a mix of excitement and nervousness. This was a crucial step in their mission to expand the GCN and make it accessible to diverse populations.

"Ready for this?" Mark asked, his voice filled with anticipation.

Emily nodded, her resolve firm. "Absolutely. Let's make this work."

They were greeted by the village leader, Mr. Patel, a kind and wise man who had been instrumental in coordinating the pilot program. He led them to the community center, where a group of villagers had gathered, curious and eager to learn about the GCN.

"Welcome, Dr. Carter, Dr. Thompson," Mr. Patel said, his smile warm. "We're excited to see what the GCN can do for our community."

"Thank you, Mr. Patel," Emily replied, shaking his hand. "We're honored to be here and look forward to working with you all."

Inside the community center, Emily and Mark set up their equipment, explaining the technology and its potential benefits to the villagers. They demonstrated how the GCN could enhance communication, foster empathy, and provide mental health support.

A young woman named Priya raised her hand, her expression curious. "How can the GCN help us with our daily lives? We have limited access to healthcare and education."

Emily smiled, appreciating the thoughtful question. "The GCN can connect you with healthcare professionals and educators from around the world. It can provide access to resources and support that might otherwise be out of reach. Our goal is to empower your community and improve your quality of life."

As the demonstration continued, the villagers began to see the potential of the GCN. They asked questions, shared their concerns, and provided valuable feedback. Emily and Mark listened intently, taking notes and adapting their approach to meet the specific needs of the community.

However, not everything went smoothly. They encountered technical issues with the network connectivity, and some villagers were skeptical about the technology's impact on their privacy and traditions.

An elderly man named Raj spoke up, his voice filled with concern. "We've lived our lives a certain way for generations. How can we be sure that this technology won't disrupt our traditions and way of life?"

Emily felt the weight of his words. "I understand your concerns, Raj. The GCN is designed to enhance your lives, not disrupt them. We want to work with you to ensure that the technology respects your traditions and values. Your feedback is crucial in helping us achieve that."

Mark added, "We're here to listen and learn. This is a partnership, and we want to make sure that the GCN is a positive addition to your community."

As the day went on, Emily and Mark worked closely with the villagers, addressing technical issues and building trust. They held workshops and training sessions, helping the community members become comfortable with the technology.

In the evening, they gathered around a bonfire, sharing stories and reflecting on the day's events. Emily felt a deep sense of connection with the villagers, their warmth and hospitality leaving a lasting impression.

"Thank you for your patience and openness," Emily said, her voice filled with gratitude. "We've learned so much from you today, and we're committed to making the GCN work for your community."

Mr. Patel smiled, his eyes reflecting the firelight. "We're grateful for your efforts, Dr. Carter. We look forward to seeing the positive impact of the GCN."

As Emily and Mark prepared to leave the village, they felt a renewed sense of purpose. The pilot program had encountered challenges, but it had also shown the potential of the GCN to make a real difference in people's lives.

Back at the research facility, they shared their experiences with the team, discussing the feedback and lessons learned. They knew that expanding the GCN would come with obstacles, but they were determined to navigate them with empathy and transparency.

"Emily, the pilot program was a success," Mark said, his voice filled with determination. "We've proven that the GCN can work in diverse communities. Now, we need to build on that success and continue to adapt our approach."

Emily nodded, her resolve strengthening. "Agreed. We'll take the feedback we've received and use it to improve the GCN. We're on the right path, but we need to keep pushing forward."

In the quiet of the research facility, surrounded by the tools of their groundbreaking work, Emily felt a renewed sense of purpose. The vision of a connected world was within reach, and with the support of their team and the commitment to ethical development, they were ready to face whatever challenges lay ahead. Together, they would make the vision of the Networked Mind a reality.

Building Partnerships

The grand hall of the international conference center was abuzz with energy as representatives from around the world gathered to discuss the future of technology and global collaboration. Dr. Emily Carter and Dr. Mark Thompson stood at the entrance, taking in the scene. This conference was a crucial opportunity to build partnerships and secure support for the expansion of the Global Consciousness Network.

"Ready for this?" Mark asked, his voice filled with anticipation.

Emily nodded, her resolve firm. "Absolutely. Let's make some connections."

They made their way through the bustling crowd, greeting familiar faces and introducing themselves to new ones. The air was thick with the hum of conversations, the exchange of ideas, and the promise of innovation. Emily felt a surge of excitement. This was their chance to showcase the GCN and its potential to foster global understanding and cooperation.

Their first meeting was with representatives from the United Nations. Emily and Mark presented the benefits of the GCN, highlighting its ability to enhance communication, provide mental health support, and bridge cultural divides.

"Dr. Carter, Dr. Thompson, the GCN is an impressive technology," said Mr. Ahmed, a senior UN official. "But there are concerns about its ethical implications and potential risks. How do you address these issues?"

Emily took a deep breath, ready to tackle the tough questions. "We understand the concerns, Mr. Ahmed. The GCN is designed with strict privacy and security measures. Each connection is encrypted, and users have full control over their level of engagement. We are also establishing an independent oversight committee to monitor the network and ensure ethical standards are upheld."

Mark added, "Our goal is to create a framework that prioritizes the safety and well-being of all users. We are committed to transparency and accountability, and we will continue to work closely with international organizations to ensure the ethical use of the GCN."

The UN representatives nodded, their expressions thoughtful. "We appreciate your commitment to ethical development. We look forward to seeing how the GCN can contribute to global cooperation."

As the day continued, Emily and Mark attended a series of meetings with potential partners from various sectors, including healthcare, education, and technology. They presented the GCN's capabilities, shared success stories from the pilot programs, and addressed any concerns raised by the attendees.

At one point, they met with Dr. Maria Santos, a renowned mental health expert from Brazil. "Dr. Carter, Dr. Thompson, the GCN has the potential to revolutionize mental health support," she said. "But how do you ensure that it is accessible to underserved communities?"

Emily smiled, appreciating the thoughtful question. "We are working closely with local organizations to tailor our approach to meet the specific needs of different communities. This includes providing culturally relevant support and ensuring that the technology is user-friendly for all populations. Our goal is to empower communities and improve their quality of life."

Dr. Santos nodded, her expression one of approval. "That's encouraging to hear. I believe the GCN can make a significant impact, and I would be interested in collaborating with you to expand its reach in Brazil."

Emily felt a surge of hope. "Thank you, Dr. Santos. We would be honored to work with you."

As the conference progressed, Emily and Mark continued to build strong partnerships and secure support for the GCN's expansion. They encountered some skepticism and resistance, but they addressed each concern with empathy and transparency, demonstrating the safeguards in place to ensure ethical use.

In the evening, they attended a networking event, where they mingled with other attendees and shared their vision for the future of the GCN. The atmosphere was one of collaboration and optimism, with people from different backgrounds and cultures coming together to discuss the potential of technology to create a better world.

"Emily, we've made some great connections today," Mark said, his voice filled with satisfaction. "The support we've received is incredible."

Emily nodded, feeling a deep sense of accomplishment. "Yes, but we still have a lot of work to do. We need to build on these partnerships and continue to adapt our approach to meet the needs of different regions."

As the event drew to a close, Emily and Mark reflected on the day's achievements. They had successfully showcased the GCN and secured valuable support for its expansion. The journey was far from over, but they were on the right path.

Back at the research facility, they shared their experiences with the team, discussing the feedback and lessons learned. They knew that expanding the GCN would come with challenges, but they were determined to navigate them with empathy and transparency.

"Emily, the conference was a success," Mark said, his voice filled with determination. "We've proven that the GCN can work in diverse communities. Now, we need to build on that success and continue to adapt our approach."

Emily nodded, her resolve strengthening. "Agreed. We'll take the feedback we've received and use it to improve the GCN. We're on the right path, but we need to keep pushing forward."

In the quiet of the research facility, surrounded by the tools of their groundbreaking work, Emily felt a renewed sense of purpose. The vision of a connected world was within reach, and with the support of their team and the commitment to ethical development, they were ready to face whatever challenges lay ahead. Together, they would make the vision of the Networked Mind a reality.

Overcoming Challenges

The research facility was a hive of activity as Dr. Emily Carter and Dr. Mark Thompson led their team in the expansion of the Global Consciousness Network. The initial success of the pilot programs had been encouraging, but the road ahead was fraught with challenges. They faced technical difficulties, logistical hurdles, and cultural barriers that required innovative solutions and unwavering determination.

Emily stood in the main lab, surrounded by monitors displaying real-time data from the new regions where the GCN had been implemented. Dr. James Lee and his cybersecurity team were hard at work, addressing technical issues and ensuring the stability of the network.

"James, how are we looking on the connectivity front?" Emily asked, her eyes scanning the screens.

James looked up, his expression focused but determined. "We've encountered some issues with the infrastructure in the rural areas. The connectivity is unstable, and we're working on optimizing the network to handle the load."

Emily nodded, her mind racing with possibilities. "Let's prioritize the regions with the most critical needs. We can deploy additional resources to strengthen the infrastructure and ensure a stable connection."

Meanwhile, in the user support center, Dr. Sarah Mitchell and her team were busy assisting users and gathering feedback. The atmosphere was one of calm efficiency, but the challenges were evident.

"Sarah, how are the users adapting to the new tools and resources?" Emily asked as she entered the room.

Sarah smiled, though her eyes showed signs of fatigue. "The feedback has been mixed. Some users are finding the technology helpful, but others are struggling with the interface and the emotional intensity of the connections. We're working on providing additional training and support."

Emily felt a deep sense of gratitude for her team's dedication. "Thank you, Sarah. Your work is making a real impact. Let's continue to gather feedback and adapt our approach to meet the users' needs."

As the team continued their efforts, they faced significant logistical challenges. In one region, the delivery of essential equipment was delayed due to transportation issues. In another, cultural resistance to the technology posed a barrier to its acceptance.

Mark, who had been coordinating with local partners, approached Emily with an update. "We've hit a snag with the equipment delivery in the northern region. The roads are in poor condition, and the trucks are having trouble getting through."

Emily sighed, feeling the weight of the obstacles pressing down on her. "Let's explore alternative transportation options. Can we use smaller vehicles or even drones to deliver the equipment?"

Mark nodded, his expression resolute. "I'll coordinate with the logistics team and see what we can do."

In another part of the facility, Emily and Mark met with local partners to address cultural resistance. They held a series of workshops and community meetings, listening to the concerns of the residents and providing clear, transparent information about the GCN and its benefits.

An elderly woman named Amina spoke up during one of the meetings, her voice filled with skepticism. "We've lived our lives a certain way for generations. How can we be sure that this technology won't disrupt our traditions and way of life?"

Emily felt the weight of her words. "I understand your concerns, Amina. The GCN is designed to enhance your lives, not disrupt them. We want to work with you to ensure that the technology respects your traditions and values. Your feedback is crucial in helping us achieve that."

Mark added, "We're here to listen and learn. This is a partnership, and we want to make sure that the GCN is a positive addition to your community."

As the days turned into nights, the team worked tirelessly to overcome the challenges. They collaborated with local partners, adapted their strategies, and found innovative solutions to the obstacles they faced. Emily felt a deep sense of pride as she watched her colleagues' resilience and determination shine through.

One evening, as the team gathered for a progress update, Ethan presented a breakthrough. "We've identified a way to optimize the network connectivity in the rural areas," he said, his eyes bright with excitement. "By using a combination of satellite and terrestrial networks, we can ensure a stable connection even in the most remote regions."

Emily felt a surge of hope. "That's incredible, Ethan. Let's start working on the implementation immediately."

As the team continued their efforts, they made significant progress in expanding the GCN. They addressed technical difficulties, navigated logistical hurdles, and built trust with the communities they served. The journey was far from over, but they were on the right path.

In the quiet moments, Emily reflected on the challenges they had faced and the lessons they had learned. The vision of a connected world, where empathy and understanding transcended barriers, was within reach.

Mark approached her, his eyes filled with a mix of exhaustion and hope. "Emily, we've got a long road ahead, but I believe in what we're doing. The GCN has the potential to change the world, and we're making it happen."

Emily smiled, feeling a renewed sense of purpose. "Thank you, Mark. I couldn't do this without you and the team. Together, we'll overcome these challenges and realize the full potential of the Networked Mind."

In the quiet of the research facility, surrounded by the tools of their groundbreaking work, Emily felt a deep sense of resolve. The journey was far from over, but with the support of her team and the commitment to ethical development, she was ready to lead the way. Together, they would make the vision of the Networked Mind a reality.

Celebrating Success

The research facility was filled with a sense of anticipation as Dr. Emily Carter and Dr. Mark Thompson prepared for the global press conference. The past few months had been a whirlwind of intense work and sleepless nights, but the team had successfully expanded the Global Consciousness Network to new regions. Today, they would celebrate their achievements and share their vision for the future with the world.

Emily stood in front of the mirror in her office, adjusting her blazer and taking a deep breath. She felt a mix of exhaustion and determination. This was their moment to show the world the positive impact of the GCN and outline their plans for continued innovation and collaboration.

Mark knocked on the door, his expression serious but supportive. "Emily, it's time. Are you ready?"

Emily nodded, her resolve strengthening. "Let's do this."

They walked together to the press conference room, where a sea of reporters and cameras awaited them. The room buzzed with anticipation, the air thick with tension. Emily and Mark took their places at the podium, the bright lights casting harsh shadows on their faces.

"Good morning," Emily began, her voice steady but filled with emotion. "Thank you all for being here. Over the past few months, we have worked tirelessly to expand the Global Consciousness Network to new regions and demographics. Today, we are here to celebrate our achievements and share our vision for the future."

The large screen behind her flickered to life, displaying a series of data points, maps, and testimonials from users around the world. Emily clicked through the slides, highlighting key achievements and milestones.

"We have successfully implemented the GCN in several new regions, including rural areas and underserved communities," Emily continued. "Our partnerships with local organizations have been crucial in ensuring that the technology is accessible and beneficial to a diverse range of users."

Mark stepped forward to provide more details. "We have also focused on enhancing the security and stability of the GCN. Our multi-layered security system and real-time monitoring capabilities have proven effective in protecting the network and ensuring a positive user experience."

A reporter raised her hand, her expression serious. "Dr. Carter, how have you addressed the cultural differences and unique needs of the new regions where the GCN has been implemented?"

Emily smiled, appreciating the thoughtful question. "We have worked closely with local partners to understand the cultural context and tailor our approach accordingly. This includes providing culturally relevant mental health resources and support, as well as ensuring that the technology is accessible and user-friendly for all populations."

Another reporter asked, "What are your plans for further expansion? How do you ensure that the GCN remains a force for good as it continues to grow?"

Mark addressed the question with confidence. "We are committed to continuous improvement and ethical development. Our independent oversight committee will monitor the GCN and ensure that it is used responsibly and for the benefit of all. We will also continue to build strong partnerships with international organizations and governments to support our expansion efforts."

The press conference continued, with Emily and Mark addressing a range of questions and sharing their vision for the future. They knew that expanding the GCN would come with challenges, but they were determined to navigate them with empathy and transparency.

As the press conference drew to a close, Emily felt a mix of exhaustion and determination. They had faced the public, acknowledged the challenges, and outlined their plan to address them. It was a crucial step forward, but the journey was far from over.

Back in her office, Emily sat down at her desk, her mind racing with the events of the day. She knew that the road ahead would be difficult, but she was ready to face whatever challenges lay ahead. With the support of her team and the commitment to ethical development, she was determined to protect the GCN and realize its full potential.

Mark entered the office, his expression serious but hopeful. "You did great today, Emily. We made it clear that we're taking this seriously and that we're committed to finding solutions."

Emily smiled, feeling a renewed sense of purpose. "Thank you, Mark. We have a lot of work to do, but I believe in the vision of the GCN. Together, we'll find a way to overcome these challenges and create a better, more connected world."

In the quiet of her office, surrounded by the tools of their groundbreaking work, Emily felt a deep sense of resolve. The journey was far from

over, but with the support of her team and the commitment to ethical development, she was ready to lead the way. Together, they would make the vision of the Networked Mind a reality.

13

CHAPTER 12: HIDDEN AGENDAS

Uncovering the Truth

The secure meeting room at the research facility was filled with a tense anticipation. Dr. Emily Carter stood at the head of the table, surrounded by her dedicated team and Ethan, the former hacker who had become an invaluable ally. The large screen behind her displayed a series of data points and profiles, each one hinting at hidden agendas within powerful organizations. Today, they would delve into these revelations and decide on their next steps.

"Thank you all for coming," Emily began, her voice steady but urgent. "We've received new information that suggests there are hidden agendas within several powerful organizations. These entities may be working against the Global Consciousness Network, and we need to uncover the truth."

Dr. James Lee, head of the cybersecurity team, leaned forward. "We've analyzed the data, and there are clear patterns that indicate coordinated efforts to undermine the GCN. These aren't isolated incidents; there's a strategy at play."

Dr. Sarah Mitchell, the neuroscientist, added, "We need to understand their motivations. Why are they targeting the GCN? What do they hope to achieve? Understanding their goals will help us anticipate their next moves."

Emily nodded, her mind racing with possibilities. "We've identified several leads that could help us trace the origins of these hidden agendas. Our goal is to gather as much information as possible and piece together the full picture."

Ethan, who had been instrumental in providing insights into the hacker group's methods, spoke up. "We need to be careful. These organizations are powerful and well-connected. If we make a wrong move, it could jeopardize everything we've worked for."

The room fell silent as the team absorbed Ethan's warning. Emily could see the conflict in their eyes, the struggle between their dedication to the project and their fear of the risks involved.

Dr. Karen Foster, the psychologist, voiced her concerns. "We need to proceed with caution. Trust is fragile, and any misstep could undermine our efforts. We should establish clear guidelines and ensure that our investigation is both thorough and ethical."

Emily appreciated Karen's caution. "You're right, Karen. We'll proceed carefully and ensure that our actions are both effective and ethical. Our priority is to protect the GCN and its users."

As the discussion continued, differing opinions emerged about the best approach to take. Some team members were eager to take bold actions and dive headfirst into the investigation, while others advocated for a more cautious and measured approach.

Dr. Lee spoke up, his tone resolute. "We can't afford to be passive. The sooner we uncover the truth, the sooner we can start making a positive impact."

Dr. Mitchell countered, "But we need to ensure that we're doing it right. Rushing the process could lead to mistakes and undermine our efforts. We need to be thorough and considerate."

Emily felt the weight of the decision pressing down on her. She understood the urgency, but she also knew that they couldn't afford to make mistakes. "We'll strike a balance. We'll be proactive, but we'll also be careful. Let's finalize our plans and ensure that everyone is prepared."

The team spent the next few hours mapping out their strategy in detail. They identified key tasks, assigned responsibilities, and established timelines. Emily and Mark would lead the efforts to follow the leads, while James and Sarah would support the investigation from the facility.

As the meeting drew to a close, Emily addressed the team one last time. "This is a critical mission. We need to uncover the truth behind these hidden agendas and protect the GCN. I have full confidence in each of you. Let's stay focused and work together."

The team members nodded, their expressions resolute. They knew the road ahead would be challenging, but they were ready to face whatever obstacles lay in their path.

In the quiet of the meeting room, surrounded by the tools of their groundbreaking work, Emily felt a renewed sense of determination. The journey was far from over, but with the support of her team and the commitment to uncovering the truth, she was ready to lead the way. Together, they would find the answers they sought and secure the future of the Networked Mind.

Following the Leads

The sun was just beginning to rise as Dr. Emily Carter and Dr. Mark Thompson set out on their mission to uncover the hidden agendas threatening the Global Consciousness Network. Their first stop was a sleek corporate office in the heart of the city, a place that exuded power and influence. Emily felt a mix of determination and apprehension as they approached the building, knowing that the stakes were high.

"Ready for this?" Mark asked, his voice steady but filled with anticipation.

Emily nodded, her resolve firm. "Absolutely. Let's find out what they're hiding."

They entered the building, their credentials granting them access to the upper floors where the executives worked. They were greeted by a polished receptionist who directed them to a conference room. Inside, they found Mr. Harrison, a high-ranking executive with a reputation for being both shrewd and secretive.

"Dr. Carter, Dr. Thompson, welcome," Mr. Harrison said, his smile not quite reaching his eyes. "What can I do for you today?"

Emily took a deep breath, choosing her words carefully. "Thank you for meeting with us, Mr. Harrison. We're here to discuss some concerns we have regarding the GCN. We've come across information that suggests there may be hidden agendas within your organization that could undermine our work."

Mr. Harrison's expression remained neutral, but Emily could sense the tension in the room. "I'm not sure what you're referring to, Dr. Carter. Our organization has always supported the GCN and its mission."

Mark stepped in, his tone calm but firm. "We've identified patterns that indicate coordinated efforts to exploit the GCN for purposes that go against its intended use. We need to understand what's going on and ensure that the network remains secure and ethical."

Mr. Harrison leaned back in his chair, his eyes narrowing slightly. "These are serious accusations. Do you have any evidence to support your claims?"

Emily and Mark exchanged a glance. They knew they had to tread carefully. "We're in the process of gathering more information," Emily said. "But we wanted to give you the opportunity to address these concerns directly."

Mr. Harrison's smile returned, but it was colder this time. "I assure you, Dr. Carter, our organization has nothing to hide. If you have any specific questions, I'll do my best to answer them."

The conversation continued, with Emily and Mark probing for more information while Mr. Harrison skillfully deflected their questions. It was clear that they wouldn't get the answers they needed here, but they had planted a seed of doubt.

As they left the corporate office, Emily felt a mix of frustration and determination. "He's hiding something, Mark. I could feel it."

Mark nodded, his expression serious. "Agreed. But we need more evidence. Let's follow the other leads and see what we can uncover."

Their next stop was a government building, where they hoped to find informants who could provide more information about the hidden agendas. They navigated the labyrinthine corridors, finally arriving at the office of Ms. Alvarez, a government official known for her integrity and willingness to speak out against corruption.

"Dr. Carter, Dr. Thompson, it's a pleasure to meet you," Ms. Alvarez said, her handshake firm. "I've heard about your work with the GCN. How can I help you?"

Emily felt a surge of hope. "Thank you for meeting with us, Ms. Alvarez. We've come across information that suggests there are hidden agendas within certain organizations that could undermine the GCN. We need your help to uncover the truth."

Ms. Alvarez's expression grew serious. "I've heard rumors about this. There are powerful entities that see the GCN as a tool for control and manipulation. They're funding research and pushing for policies that would give them unprecedented access to people's minds."

Emily's heart raced. "Do you have any evidence or leads that we can follow?"

Ms. Alvarez nodded. "I can connect you with some informants who have insider knowledge. But be careful. These people are powerful and dangerous. If they find out what you're doing, they won't hesitate to retaliate."

Emily and Mark thanked Ms. Alvarez and left the building, their minds racing with the implications of what they had learned. They had a new mission now—to follow the leads and uncover the truth behind the hidden agendas.

As they continued their investigation, they encountered resistance and mistrust from potential informants. They had to use their negotiation skills and leverage their knowledge to gain the trust of key individuals. The investigation became increasingly dangerous as they got closer to the truth.

One evening, as they met with a potential informant in a dimly lit café, Emily felt the weight of the risks they were taking. "We need to be careful, Mark. We're getting close, but we can't afford to make any mistakes."

Mark nodded, his expression resolute. "I know, Emily. But we have to see this through. The future of the GCN depends on it."

In the quiet of the café, surrounded by the shadows of uncertainty, Emily felt a renewed sense of determination. The journey was far from over, but with the support of her team and the commitment to uncovering the truth, she was ready to lead the way. Together, they would find the answers they sought and secure the future of the Networked Mind.

The Revelation

The night was dark and cold as Dr. Emily Carter and Dr. Mark Thompson arrived at a remote location on the outskirts of the city. The address they had been given led them to an abandoned warehouse, its windows boarded up and the surrounding area eerily quiet. Emily felt a mix of anticipation and apprehension. This clandestine meeting with a key informant could provide the breakthrough they needed to uncover the hidden agendas threatening the Global Consciousness Network.

"Are you sure about this, Emily?" Mark asked, his voice low and cautious. "This could be dangerous."

Emily nodded, her resolve unwavering. "We need to know the truth, Mark. This might be our only chance."

They approached the entrance, a heavy metal door that creaked ominously as they pushed it open. Inside, the warehouse was dimly lit, the air thick with the scent of dust and oil. They moved cautiously through the shadows, their footsteps echoing softly on the concrete floor.

"Stay close," Emily whispered, her eyes scanning the darkened space for any signs of movement.

As they ventured deeper into the warehouse, they spotted a lone figure standing by a table, illuminated by the faint glow of a single lamp. The informant, a man in his late forties with a weathered face and wary eyes, looked up as they approached.

"Dr. Carter, Dr. Thompson," he said, his voice low and gravelly. "I'm glad you came. We don't have much time."

Emily and Mark exchanged a glance, then stepped forward, their presence immediately noticed by the informant. "Thank you for meeting with us," Emily said, her voice steady. "We need to understand what's going on and who is behind these attacks on the GCN."

The informant nodded, his expression serious. "I've been working on the inside for years, gathering information. There are powerful entities—corporations and government agencies—that see the GCN as a tool for control and manipulation. They're funding research and pushing for policies that would give them unprecedented access to people's minds."

Emily felt a chill run down her spine. "What do they hope to achieve?"

The informant's eyes darkened. "They want to use the GCN to monitor and influence people's thoughts and behaviors. It's about power and control. They see the GCN as a way to shape society according to their own agendas."

Mark's jaw tightened. "Do you have any evidence to support these claims?"

The informant reached into his coat and pulled out a flash drive. "Everything you need is on here. Emails, documents, recordings—proof of their plans and the people involved. But be careful. These are powerful and dangerous people. If they find out what you're doing, they won't hesitate to retaliate."

Emily took the flash drive, her heart pounding with a mix of fear and determination. "Thank you. We'll make sure this information gets out."

The informant nodded, his expression grim. "Good luck. You're going to need it."

As they left the warehouse, Emily and Mark felt the weight of the revelation pressing down on them. They had the evidence they needed, but they also knew that exposing these hidden agendas would be fraught with danger.

Back at the research facility, they gathered the team to share what they had learned. The room was filled with a tense silence as Emily inserted the flash drive into the computer and brought up the files.

"This is it," Emily said, her voice steady but filled with emotion. "This is the proof we've been looking for."

The team pored over the documents, their expressions a mix of shock and anger. The evidence was damning, revealing a web of deceit and manipulation that threatened the very foundation of the GCN.

Dr. James Lee, head of the cybersecurity team, spoke up. "We need to act fast. We can't let these entities continue to exploit the GCN for their own gain."

Dr. Sarah Mitchell, the neuroscientist, added, "We also need to protect ourselves. If they find out what we know, they'll come after us."

Emily nodded, her resolve strengthening. "We'll be careful. But we can't let fear stop us from doing what's right. We need to expose these hidden agendas and ensure that the GCN remains a force for good."

As the team continued to analyze the evidence and develop their strategy, Emily felt a renewed sense of purpose. The journey was far from over, but with the support of her team and the commitment to uncovering the truth, she was ready to lead the way.

In the quiet of the research facility, surrounded by the tools of their groundbreaking work, Emily felt a deep sense of resolve. Together, they would find the answers they sought and secure the future of the Networked Mind.

Confronting the Adversaries

The research facility's secure conference room was filled with a charged atmosphere as Dr. Emily Carter and Dr. Mark Thompson prepared to confront representatives from the powerful organizations implicated in the hidden agendas. The evidence they had gathered was damning, and today, they would demand accountability. Emily felt a mix of determination and apprehension as she reviewed the documents one last time.

"Are you ready for this?" Mark asked, his voice steady but filled with anticipation.

Emily nodded, her resolve firm. "Absolutely. It's time to hold them accountable."

The room was arranged with a long conference table, at one end of which sat Emily, Mark, and their core team, including Dr. James Lee and Dr. Sarah Mitchell. At the other end were the representatives from the implicated organizations, their expressions a mix of confidence and wariness. Among them was Mr. Harrison, the corporate executive they had previously met, and Ms. Alvarez, the government official who had initially helped them.

"Thank you all for coming," Emily began, her voice steady but firm. "We have gathered substantial evidence that suggests coordinated efforts to undermine the Global Consciousness Network. These efforts are not only unethical but also pose a significant threat to the integrity and purpose of the GCN."

Mr. Harrison leaned back in his chair, his expression neutral. "These are serious accusations, Dr. Carter. What evidence do you have to support these claims?"

Emily took a deep breath and began presenting the evidence. The large screen behind her displayed emails, documents, and recordings that detailed the hidden agendas and the entities involved. The room fell silent as the representatives absorbed the gravity of the revelations.

"This evidence shows a clear pattern of manipulation and exploitation," Emily continued. "These entities have been funding research and pushing for policies that would give them unprecedented access to people's minds. Their goal is to use the GCN to monitor and influence thoughts and behaviors for their own gain."

Ms. Alvarez, who had initially seemed supportive, now looked visibly uncomfortable. "Dr. Carter, these are serious allegations. Are you certain of the authenticity of this evidence?"

Mark stepped in, his tone calm but resolute. "We have verified the authenticity of the evidence through multiple sources. The documents and recordings are genuine, and they paint a disturbing picture of the intentions behind these actions."

The representatives from the implicated organizations began to murmur among themselves, their confidence wavering. Mr. Harrison, however, remained composed. "This is a complex issue, Dr. Carter. Even if these documents are genuine, it doesn't necessarily mean that our intentions were malicious. We have always supported the GCN and its mission."

Emily felt a surge of frustration but kept her composure. "The evidence speaks for itself, Mr. Harrison. These actions are not in line with the ethical principles that the GCN was founded on. We demand accountability and transparency."

The confrontation grew more intense as both sides presented their arguments and defended their positions. The representatives from the implicated organizations attempted to discredit the team's findings, but Emily and her team remained steadfast, presenting irrefutable evidence to support their claims.

Dr. James Lee, head of the cybersecurity team, spoke up. "The integrity of the GCN is at stake. We cannot allow it to be used as a tool for control and manipulation. We need to ensure that it remains a force for good, fostering empathy and understanding."

Dr. Sarah Mitchell added, "We have a responsibility to protect the users of the GCN and ensure that their thoughts and emotions are not exploited. This is about more than just technology; it's about human dignity and ethical responsibility."

As the confrontation continued, the representatives from the implicated organizations began to show signs of capitulation. The weight of the evidence and the determination of Emily and her team were undeniable.

Finally, Mr. Harrison spoke, his tone more conciliatory. "Dr. Carter, Dr. Thompson, we understand your concerns. We are willing to cooperate and work towards a solution that ensures the ethical use of the GCN. Let's find a way to move forward together."

Emily felt a sense of relief but knew that the journey was far from over. "Thank you, Mr. Harrison. We appreciate your willingness to cooperate. Our goal is to ensure that the GCN remains a force for good, and we will work tirelessly to achieve that."

As the meeting drew to a close, Emily and her team felt a renewed sense of purpose. They had confronted the adversaries and demanded accountability, but there was still much work to be done.

Back in her office, Emily sat down at her desk, her mind racing with the events of the day. She knew that the road ahead would be difficult, but she was ready to face whatever challenges lay ahead. With the support of her team and the commitment to ethical development, she was determined to protect the GCN and realize its full potential.

Mark entered the office, his expression serious but hopeful. "You did great today, Emily. We made it clear that we're taking this seriously and that we're committed to finding solutions."

Emily smiled, feeling a renewed sense of purpose. "Thank you, Mark. We have a lot of work to do, but I believe in the vision of the GCN. Together, we'll find a way to overcome these challenges and create a better, more connected world."

In the quiet of her office, surrounded by the tools of their groundbreaking work, Emily felt a deep sense of resolve. The journey was far from over, but with the support of her team and the commitment to ethical development, she was ready to lead the way. Together, they would make the vision of the Networked Mind a reality.

A Path Forward

The research facility was quiet, the hum of the equipment a comforting backdrop as Dr. Emily Carter and Dr. Mark Thompson gathered their team in Emily's office. The recent confrontation with the powerful organizations had been intense, but they had managed to hold their ground and demand accountability. Now, it was time to reflect on their journey and plan their next steps.

Emily stood at the head of the table, her eyes scanning the faces of her dedicated team. She could see the exhaustion etched into their expressions, but she also saw the spark of determination that had carried them through the crisis.

"Thank you all for being here," Emily began, her voice steady but filled with emotion. "We've faced incredible challenges over the past few weeks, but we've also made significant progress. I wanted to take a moment to acknowledge your hard work and dedication. Your efforts have made a real difference, and I couldn't be prouder to work alongside you."

Dr. James Lee, head of the cybersecurity team, leaned forward. "We've enhanced the security of the GCN and implemented a multi-layered system that adapts to new threats in real-time. The recent attack was a testament to our resilience and our ability to protect the network."

Dr. Sarah Mitchell, the neuroscientist, added, "We've also expanded our mental health resources and support groups, providing users with the tools they need to manage their emotional responses. The feedback from users has been overwhelmingly positive."

Ethan, the former hacker who had joined their efforts, spoke up. "We've made great strides in securing the GCN, but we need to stay vigilant. The hacker group won't give up easily, and we need to be prepared for future challenges."

Emily nodded, her mind racing with the implications of their work. "You're right, Ethan. We need to stay focused and continue to improve the GCN. But I also want to acknowledge the personal sacrifices each of you has made. Your dedication and resilience have been truly inspiring."

Mark, who had been coordinating with external experts, spoke up. "We've also built strong partnerships with leading cybersecurity firms and mental health organizations. Their expertise has been invaluable, and we need to continue to collaborate with them to ensure the GCN remains a force for good."

The room fell silent as the team absorbed the gravity of their journey. Despite their victory, doubts and fears lingered. Emily could see the uncertainty in their eyes, and she knew she needed to inspire them to continue their work.

"Everyone, I know this has been a difficult journey," Emily said, her voice filled with conviction. "But we've proven that we can overcome incredible challenges. The GCN has the potential to change the world, and we are the ones who will make that happen. We need to believe in our vision and stay committed to our mission."

Dr. Karen Foster, the psychologist, nodded in agreement. "We've learned valuable lessons along the way. We've seen the importance of ethical development and the need to prioritize the well-being of our users. These principles will guide us as we move forward."

Emily felt a deep sense of pride as she looked around the room. "Thank you, Karen. And thank you, everyone. Your hard work and dedication have brought us to this point. Let's continue to work together and make the GCN a tool for empathy, understanding, and connection."

As the meeting drew to a close, the team members exchanged words of encouragement and support. They knew the road ahead would be challenging, but they were ready to face whatever obstacles lay in their path.

In the quiet of her office, surrounded by the tools of their groundbreaking work, Emily felt a renewed sense of resolve. The journey was far from over, but with the support of her team and the commitment to ethical development, she was ready to lead the way. Together, they would secure the future of the Networked Mind and ensure that it remained a force for good.

Later that evening, Emily sat at her desk, reflecting on the day's events. She knew that the road ahead would be difficult, but she was ready to face whatever challenges lay ahead. With the support of her team and the commitment to ethical development, she was determined to protect the GCN and realize its full potential.

Mark entered the office, his expression serious but hopeful. "You did great today, Emily. We made it clear that we're taking this seriously and that we're committed to finding solutions."

Emily smiled, feeling a renewed sense of purpose. "Thank you, Mark. We have a lot of work to do, but I believe in the vision of the GCN. Together, we'll find a way to overcome these challenges and create a better, more connected world."

In the quiet of her office, surrounded by the tools of their groundbreaking work, Emily felt a deep sense of resolve. The journey was far from over, but with the support of her team and the commitment to ethical development, she was ready to lead the way. Together, they would make the vision of the Networked Mind a reality.

14

CHAPTER 13: THE RESISTANCE

The Emergence of the Resistance

The secure meeting room at the research facility was filled with a palpable tension. Dr. Emily Carter stood at the head of the table, surrounded by her dedicated team and Ethan, the former hacker who had become an invaluable ally. The large screen behind her displayed a series of data points and profiles, each one hinting at the emergence of a resistance group that opposed the Global Consciousness Network. Today, they would delve into these revelations and decide on their next steps.

"Thank you all for coming," Emily began, her voice steady but urgent. "We've received new information that suggests a resistance group has formed to oppose the GCN. We need to understand their motives and strategies, and assess the potential impact on our work."

Dr. James Lee, head of the cybersecurity team, leaned forward. "We've analyzed the data, and there are clear indications that this group is well-organized and determined. They see the GCN as a threat to privacy and individual freedom."

Dr. Sarah Mitchell, the neuroscientist, added, "We need to understand their concerns. Why are they so opposed to the GCN? What do they hope to achieve? Understanding their perspective will help us address their grievances."

Emily nodded, her mind racing with possibilities. "We've identified several leads that could help us trace the origins of this resistance group. Our goal is to gather as much information as possible and find a way to address their concerns."

Ethan, who had been instrumental in providing insights into the hacker group's methods, spoke up. "We need to be careful. This group is likely to be suspicious and hostile. If we approach them the wrong way, it could escalate the situation."

The room fell silent as the team absorbed Ethan's warning. Emily could see the conflict in their eyes, the struggle between their dedication to the project and their fear of the risks involved.

Dr. Karen Foster, the psychologist, voiced her concerns. "We need to proceed with caution. Trust is fragile, and any misstep could undermine our efforts. We should establish clear guidelines and ensure that our approach is both strategic and empathetic."

Emily appreciated Karen's caution. "You're right, Karen. We'll proceed carefully and ensure that our actions are both effective and ethical. Our priority is to protect the GCN and its users."

As the discussion continued, differing opinions emerged about the best approach to take. Some team members were eager to take bold actions and confront the resistance head-on, while others advocated for a more cautious and dialogue-driven approach.

Dr. Lee spoke up, his tone resolute. "We can't afford to be passive. The sooner we understand their motives, the sooner we can address their concerns and prevent any potential sabotage."

Dr. Mitchell countered, "But we need to ensure that we're doing it right. Rushing the process could lead to mistakes and further alienate the resistance. We need to be thorough and considerate."

Emily felt the weight of the decision pressing down on her. She understood the urgency, but she also knew that they couldn't afford to make mistakes. "We'll strike a balance. We'll be proactive, but we'll also be careful. Let's finalize our plans and ensure that everyone is prepared."

The team spent the next few hours mapping out their strategy in detail. They identified key tasks, assigned responsibilities, and established timelines. Emily and Mark would lead the efforts to infiltrate the resistance, while James and Sarah would support the investigation from the facility.

As the meeting drew to a close, Emily addressed the team one last time. "This is a critical mission. We need to understand the resistance's concerns and find a way to address them. I have full confidence in each of you. Let's stay focused and work together."

The team members nodded, their expressions resolute. They knew the road ahead would be challenging, but they were ready to face whatever obstacles lay in their path.

In the quiet of the meeting room, surrounded by the tools of their groundbreaking work, Emily felt a renewed sense of determination. The journey was far from over, but with the support of her team and the commitment to understanding and addressing the resistance's concerns, she was ready to lead the way. Together, they would find the answers they sought and secure the future of the Networked Mind.

Infiltrating the Resistance

The night was dark and filled with an air of secrecy as Dr. Emily Carter, Dr. Mark Thompson, and Ethan prepared to infiltrate the resistance group.

They had spent days gathering intel and planning their approach, and now it was time to put their plan into action. The resistance had been organizing underground meetings and using online forums to coordinate their efforts, and Emily knew that understanding their concerns was crucial to addressing the opposition to the Global Consciousness Network.

"Are you ready for this?" Mark asked, his voice low but steady.

Emily nodded, her resolve firm. "We need to know what they're planning. Let's do this."

They arrived at a nondescript building on the outskirts of the city, the location of one of the resistance's underground meetings. The building was old and worn, its windows covered with grime. Emily felt a mix of anticipation and apprehension as they approached the entrance.

Ethan, who had experience with such covert operations, led the way. "Remember, we're here to gather information and understand their perspective. Stay calm and blend in."

They entered the building, their presence immediately noticed by the group of people gathered inside. The room was dimly lit, filled with the murmur of hushed conversations. Emily and Mark exchanged a glance, then followed Ethan's lead as he approached a group of individuals who seemed to be the organizers.

"Evening," Ethan said, his voice casual. "We're here to learn more about what you're doing. We share your concerns about the GCN."

One of the organizers, a woman with sharp eyes and a guarded demeanor, looked them over. "Who are you? We don't recognize you."

Emily stepped forward, her voice steady. "We're concerned citizens who believe in the importance of privacy and individual freedom. We've heard about your efforts and wanted to learn more."

The woman studied them for a moment, then nodded. "Alright. But keep your heads down and listen. We're not here to make friends."

As the meeting continued, Emily and Mark listened intently, taking mental notes of the group's concerns and strategies. The resistance members spoke passionately about their fears of the GCN being used for surveillance and control, and their determination to protect their privacy and autonomy.

"We can't let them control our thoughts and emotions," one man said, his voice filled with conviction. "The GCN is a tool for manipulation, and we need to fight back."

Emily felt a pang of empathy. She understood their fears, even if she didn't agree with their methods. She knew that addressing these concerns was crucial to finding a path forward.

After the meeting, Emily, Mark, and Ethan retreated to a quiet corner to discuss their observations. "They're well-organized and determined," Mark said, his voice low. "But their concerns are based on misinformation and fear."

Ethan nodded. "We need to find a way to address their fears and show them that the GCN can be a force for good."

Their next step was to infiltrate the online forums where the resistance coordinated their efforts. Using aliases, they joined the discussions, posing as sympathizers to gather more information. The forums were filled with heated debates and conspiracy theories, but also genuine concerns about privacy and autonomy.

Emily and Mark engaged in the discussions, carefully steering the conversation to gather insights into the resistance's plans and motivations. They encountered suspicion and hostility, but their persistence paid off as they gained the trust of key individuals.

One evening, as they participated in an online discussion, a user named "Shadow" reached out to them privately. "You seem to understand our concerns. We need people like you to help us fight back."

Emily felt a surge of anticipation. "We're here to help. What do you need?"

Shadow provided them with information about an upcoming meeting with the resistance leaders. "This is our chance to make a real impact. We need to be prepared."

Emily and Mark knew that this meeting could be the turning point in their investigation. They needed to understand the resistance's perspective and find a way to address their concerns.

As they prepared for the meeting, Emily felt a mix of determination and apprehension. The journey was far from over, but with the support of her team and the commitment to understanding and addressing the resistance's concerns, she was ready to lead the way.

In the quiet of their temporary base, surrounded by the tools of their covert operation, Emily felt a deep sense of resolve. Together, they would find the answers they sought and secure the future of the Networked Mind.

The Turning Point

The night was cold and still as Dr. Emily Carter, Dr. Mark Thompson, and Ethan arrived at the remote location for their clandestine meeting with the leaders of the resistance. The address they had been given led them to an old, abandoned warehouse on the outskirts of the city. The building loomed in the darkness, its windows boarded up and the surrounding area eerily quiet. Emily felt a mix of anticipation and apprehension. This meeting could be the turning point in their efforts to understand and address the resistance's concerns.

"Are you sure about this, Emily?" Mark asked, his voice low and cautious. "This could be dangerous."

Emily nodded, her resolve unwavering. "We need to know the truth, Mark. This might be our only chance."

They approached the entrance, a heavy metal door that creaked ominously as they pushed it open. Inside, the warehouse was dimly lit, the air thick with the scent of dust and oil. They moved cautiously through the shadows, their footsteps echoing softly on the concrete floor.

"Stay close," Emily whispered, her eyes scanning the darkened space for any signs of movement.

As they ventured deeper into the warehouse, they spotted a group of figures huddled around a table, illuminated by the faint glow of a single lamp. The leaders of the resistance looked up as they approached, their expressions a mix of suspicion and curiosity.

"Dr. Carter, Dr. Thompson," said a man with a stern face and piercing eyes. "We've been expecting you."

Emily took a deep breath, choosing her words carefully. "Thank you for meeting with us. We're here to understand your concerns and find a way to address them."

The man, who appeared to be the leader, studied them for a moment before nodding. "Very well. But know this—we don't trust easily. You'll need to prove that you're here in good faith."

Emily and Mark exchanged a glance, then stepped forward, their presence immediately noticed by the resistance leaders. "We understand your concerns," Emily said, her voice steady. "The GCN was created to foster empathy and understanding, not to control or manipulate. We want to work with you to ensure that it remains a force for good."

The leader's eyes narrowed. "Words are easy, Dr. Carter. But actions speak louder. We've seen how technology can be used to invade privacy and control people's lives. How can we be sure that the GCN won't be used in the same way?"

Mark stepped in, his tone calm but resolute. "We have implemented strict privacy and security measures to protect users. Each connection is encrypted, and participants have full control over their level of engagement. We are also establishing an independent oversight committee to monitor the network and ensure ethical standards are upheld."

The leader's expression remained skeptical. "And what about the powerful entities that see the GCN as a tool for control? How do you plan to stop them?"

Emily felt a surge of determination. "We have already confronted some of these entities and demanded accountability. We are committed to transparency and ethical development. But we need your help. We need to understand your perspective and work together to protect the GCN."

The room fell silent as the resistance leaders absorbed Emily's words. The tension was palpable, but Emily could see a flicker of hope in their eyes.

A woman with a determined expression spoke up. "We've been fighting for our privacy and autonomy for a long time. If you're serious about working with us, you'll need to prove it."

Emily nodded. "We understand. Let's start by addressing your specific concerns. What are the main issues you have with the GCN, and how can we work together to resolve them?"

The leaders began to outline their fears and grievances, from concerns about data privacy to the potential for misuse by powerful entities. Emily and Mark listened intently, taking notes and asking questions to gain a deeper understanding of their perspective.

As the meeting continued, the atmosphere began to shift. The resistance leaders, initially guarded and distrustful, started to open up. Emily could see that their fears were genuine and deeply rooted, and she knew that addressing these concerns was crucial to finding a path forward.

"We want to ensure that the GCN is used ethically and responsibly," Emily said, her voice filled with conviction. "We believe that by working together, we can create a framework that protects privacy and autonomy while fostering empathy and understanding."

The leader nodded slowly. "It's a start. But actions speak louder than words. We'll be watching closely."

Emily felt a sense of relief but knew that the journey was far from over. "Thank you for giving us this opportunity. We are committed to working with you to ensure that the GCN remains a force for good."

As the meeting drew to a close, Emily, Mark, and Ethan felt a renewed sense of purpose. They had taken the first step in building a dialogue with the resistance, but there was still much work to be done.

Back at the research facility, they shared their experiences with the team, discussing the insights they had gained and the challenges that lay ahead. They knew that bridging the divide with the resistance would be difficult, but they were determined to navigate it with empathy and transparency.

"Emily, the meeting was a success," Mark said, his voice filled with determination. "We've proven that we can engage in dialogue and find common ground. Now, we need to build on that success and continue to address their concerns."

Emily nodded, her resolve strengthening. "Agreed. We'll take the feedback we've received and use it to improve the GCN. We're on the right path, but we need to keep pushing forward."

In the quiet of the research facility, surrounded by the tools of their groundbreaking work, Emily felt a renewed sense of purpose. The vision of a connected world was within reach, and with the support of their team and the commitment to ethical development, they were ready to face whatever challenges lay ahead. Together, they would make the vision of the Networked Mind a reality.

Bridging the Divide

The research facility's secure conference room was filled with a mix of anticipation and tension as Dr. Emily Carter and Dr. Mark Thompson prepared to meet with representatives from the resistance. This series of dialogues aimed at bridging the divide between the GCN team and the resistance was crucial. Emily knew that finding common ground and addressing the resistance's concerns was essential for the future of the Global Consciousness Network.

"Are you ready for this?" Mark asked, his voice steady but filled with anticipation.

Emily nodded, her resolve firm. "Absolutely. It's time to build a bridge."

The room was arranged with a long conference table, at one end of which sat Emily, Mark, and their core team, including Dr. James Lee and Dr. Sarah Mitchell. At the other end were the representatives from the resistance, their expressions a mix of skepticism and curiosity. Among them was the leader they had met in the warehouse, his stern face now slightly softened by the willingness to engage in dialogue.

"Thank you all for coming," Emily began, her voice steady but warm. "We appreciate your willingness to meet with us. Our goal today is to listen to your concerns, discuss the ethical implications of the GCN, and explore ways to address them."

The leader of the resistance, who introduced himself as David, nodded. "We appreciate the opportunity to speak with you, Dr. Carter. Our concerns are genuine, and we hope you will take them seriously."

Emily felt a surge of determination. "We absolutely will, David. Let's start by discussing your main concerns. What are the key issues you have with the GCN, and how can we work together to resolve them?"

David leaned forward, his expression serious. "Our primary concern is privacy. The GCN has the potential to invade people's private thoughts and emotions. We fear that it could be used for surveillance and control by powerful entities."

Dr. James Lee, head of the cybersecurity team, spoke up. "We understand your concerns, David. We've implemented strict privacy and security measures to protect users. Each connection is encrypted, and participants have full control over their level of engagement. We are also establishing an independent oversight committee to monitor the network and ensure ethical standards are upheld."

A woman named Lisa, another representative from the resistance, added, "We also worry about the potential for misuse. Even with safeguards in place, how can we be sure that the GCN won't be exploited by those with malicious intent?"

Dr. Sarah Mitchell, the neuroscientist, responded, "We are committed to transparency and accountability. The oversight committee will include representatives from various sectors, including ethics, law, and human rights. Our goal is to create a framework that prioritizes the safety and well-being of all users."

The discussions were heated and emotional, with both sides struggling to find common ground. Emily could see the deep-seated fears and grievances in the eyes of the resistance representatives. She knew that addressing these concerns was crucial to building trust.

"David, Lisa, we hear you," Emily said, her voice filled with empathy. "Your concerns are valid, and we are committed to addressing them. We want to work with you to ensure that the GCN remains a force for good, fostering empathy and understanding while protecting privacy and autonomy."

David's expression softened slightly. "We appreciate your willingness to listen, Dr. Carter. But actions speak louder than words. We need to see concrete steps being taken to address our concerns."

Emily nodded. "Absolutely. Let's outline a plan together. We can start by involving your representatives in the oversight committee and working on joint initiatives to enhance privacy and security. We also want to hear your ideas on how we can improve the GCN."

As the dialogue continued, the atmosphere began to shift. The resistance representatives, initially guarded and distrustful, started to open up. Emily could see that their fears were genuine and deeply rooted, and she knew that addressing these concerns was crucial to finding a path forward.

"We want to ensure that the GCN is used ethically and responsibly," Emily said, her voice filled with conviction. "We believe that by working together, we can create a framework that protects privacy and autonomy while fostering empathy and understanding."

The leader, David, nodded slowly. "It's a start. But we'll be watching closely. We need to see real change."

Emily felt a sense of relief but knew that the journey was far from over. "Thank you for giving us this opportunity. We are committed to working with you to ensure that the GCN remains a force for good."

As the meeting drew to a close, Emily, Mark, and their team felt a renewed sense of purpose. They had taken the first step in building a dialogue with the resistance, but there was still much work to be done.

Back at the research facility, they shared their experiences with the team, discussing the insights they had gained and the challenges that lay ahead. They knew that bridging the divide with the resistance would be difficult, but they were determined to navigate it with empathy and transparency.

"Emily, the meeting was a success," Mark said, his voice filled with determination. "We've proven that we can engage in dialogue and find common ground. Now, we need to build on that success and continue to address their concerns."

Emily nodded, her resolve strengthening. "Agreed. We'll take the feedback we've received and use it to improve the GCN. We're on the right path, but we need to keep pushing forward."

In the quiet of the research facility, surrounded by the tools of their groundbreaking work, Emily felt a renewed sense of purpose. The vision of a connected world was within reach, and with the support of their team and the commitment to ethical development, they were ready to face whatever challenges lay ahead. Together, they would make the vision of the Networked Mind a reality.

A New Alliance

The research facility was abuzz with anticipation as Dr. Emily Carter and Dr. Mark Thompson prepared for the global press conference. The past few weeks had been a whirlwind of intense dialogue and negotiation, but they had finally formed a new alliance with the resistance group. Today, they would share this groundbreaking collaboration with the world and outline their shared vision for the future of the Global Consciousness Network.

Emily stood in front of the mirror in her office, adjusting her blazer and taking a deep breath. She felt a mix of exhaustion and determination. This was their moment to show the world that they were committed to ethical development and transparency.

Mark knocked on the door, his expression serious but supportive. "Emily, it's time. Are you ready?"

Emily nodded, her resolve strengthening. "Let's do this."

They walked together to the press conference room, where a sea of reporters and cameras awaited them. The room buzzed with anticipation, the air thick with tension. Emily and Mark took their places at the podium, the bright lights casting harsh shadows on their faces. Beside them stood David and Lisa, the leaders of the resistance, their expressions a mix of determination and hope.

"Good morning," Emily began, her voice steady but filled with emotion. "Thank you all for being here. Over the past few weeks, we have engaged in intense dialogue and negotiation with the resistance group. Today, we are proud to announce a new alliance that aims to ensure the ethical development and use of the Global Consciousness Network."

The large screen behind her flickered to life, displaying a series of data points, maps, and testimonials from users around the world. Emily clicked through the slides, highlighting key achievements and milestones.

"We have listened to the concerns of the resistance and have worked together to address them," Emily continued. "Our goal is to create a framework that protects privacy and autonomy while fostering empathy and understanding. This alliance is a testament to our commitment to transparency and ethical development."

Mark stepped forward to provide more details. "We have implemented new privacy and security measures, established an independent oversight committee, and involved representatives from the resistance in our decision-making process. We believe that by working together, we can create a better, more connected world."

A reporter raised her hand, her expression serious. "Dr. Carter, how can you reassure the public that this alliance will address the concerns about privacy and misuse of the GCN?"

Emily took a deep breath, her resolve unwavering. "We understand the public's concerns, and we are committed to addressing them. The oversight committee will include representatives from various sectors, including ethics, law, and human rights. Our goal is to ensure that the GCN is used responsibly and for the benefit of all."

David, the leader of the resistance, stepped forward. "We have been fighting for our privacy and autonomy for a long time. This alliance is a step in the right direction. We will be watching closely to ensure that the GCN remains a force for good."

Another reporter asked, "What are your plans for further collaboration? How do you ensure that the GCN continues to evolve ethically?"

Mark addressed the question with confidence. "We are committed to continuous improvement and ethical development. We will work closely with the oversight committee and external experts to ensure that the GCN remains a force for good. Our focus is on fostering empathy and understanding, and we will do everything in our power to protect that vision."

The press conference continued, with Emily, Mark, David, and Lisa addressing a range of questions and sharing their vision for the future. They knew that rebuilding public trust would take time and consistent effort, but they were determined to show their commitment to making the GCN safe and beneficial for everyone.

As the press conference drew to a close, Emily felt a mix of exhaustion and determination. They had faced the public, acknowledged the challenges, and outlined their plan to address them. It was a crucial step forward, but the journey was far from over.

Back in her office, Emily sat down at her desk, her mind racing with the events of the day. She knew that the road ahead would be difficult, but she was ready to face whatever challenges lay ahead. With the support of her team and the commitment to ethical development, she was determined to protect the GCN and realize its full potential.

Mark entered the office, his expression serious but hopeful. "You did great today, Emily. We made it clear that we're taking this seriously and that we're committed to finding solutions."

Emily smiled, feeling a renewed sense of purpose. "Thank you, Mark. We have a lot of work to do, but I believe in the vision of the GCN. Together, we'll find a way to overcome these challenges and create a better, more connected world."

In the quiet of her office, surrounded by the tools of their groundbreaking work, Emily felt a deep sense of resolve. The journey was far from over, but with the support of her team and the commitment to ethical development, she was ready to lead the way. Together, they would make the vision of the Networked Mind a reality.

15

CHAPTER 14: THE FINAL SHOWDOWN

The Discovery

The research facility was bathed in the soft glow of computer screens as Dr. Emily Carter and her team worked late into the night. The air was thick with tension and urgency. They had just discovered a critical vulnerability in the Global Consciousness Network, one that their adversaries were planning to exploit. The stakes had never been higher.

Emily stood in the secure lab, surrounded by her dedicated team and Ethan, the former hacker who had become an invaluable ally. The large screen behind her displayed a series of data points and code, each one highlighting the severity of the threat they faced.

"Thank you all for coming," Emily began, her voice steady but urgent. "We've identified a critical vulnerability in the GCN that our adversaries plan to exploit. This could have catastrophic consequences if we don't act quickly."

Dr. James Lee, head of the cybersecurity team, leaned forward, his expression grim. "We've analyzed the data, and it's clear that this vulnerability could allow them to gain control over the network. We need to develop a countermeasure immediately."

Dr. Sarah Mitchell, the neuroscientist, added, "The psychological impact on users could be devastating. We need to ensure that the GCN remains secure and that our users are protected."

Emily nodded, her mind racing with possibilities. "We've identified several potential solutions, but we need to act fast. Our goal is to develop a countermeasure and implement it before the adversaries can launch their attack."

Ethan, who had been instrumental in providing insights into the hacker group's methods, spoke up. "We need to be careful. This group is highly skilled and well-funded. If we make a wrong move, it could jeopardize everything we've worked for."

The room fell silent as the team absorbed Ethan's warning. Emily could see the conflict in their eyes, the struggle between their dedication to the project and their fear of the risks involved.

Dr. Karen Foster, the psychologist, voiced her concerns. "We need to proceed with caution. Trust is fragile, and any misstep could undermine our efforts. We should establish clear guidelines and ensure that our approach is both strategic and empathetic."

Emily appreciated Karen's caution. "You're right, Karen. We'll proceed carefully and ensure that our actions are both effective and ethical. Our priority is to protect the GCN and its users."

As the discussion continued, differing opinions emerged about the best approach to take. Some team members were eager to take bold actions and confront the adversaries head-on, while others advocated for a more cautious and measured approach.

Dr. Lee spoke up, his tone resolute. "We can't afford to be passive. The sooner we develop a countermeasure, the sooner we can prevent the attack and protect the GCN."

Dr. Mitchell countered, "But we need to ensure that we're doing it right. Rushing the process could lead to mistakes and undermine our efforts. We need to be thorough and considerate."

Emily felt the weight of the decision pressing down on her. She understood the urgency, but she also knew that they couldn't afford to make mistakes. "We'll strike a balance. We'll be proactive, but we'll also be careful. Let's finalize our plans and ensure that everyone is prepared."

The team spent the next few hours mapping out their strategy in detail. They identified key tasks, assigned responsibilities, and established timelines. Emily and Mark would oversee the overall implementation, while James and Sarah would lead the efforts in their respective areas.

As the meeting drew to a close, Emily addressed the team one last time. "This is a critical mission. We need to develop a countermeasure and protect the GCN. I have full confidence in each of you. Let's stay focused and work together."

The team members nodded, their expressions resolute. They knew the road ahead would be challenging, but they were ready to face whatever obstacles lay in their path.

In the quiet of the secure lab, surrounded by the tools of their groundbreaking work, Emily felt a renewed sense of determination. The journey was far from over, but with the support of her team and the commitment to protecting the GCN, she was ready to lead the way. Together, they would find the answers they sought and secure the future of the Networked Mind.

Preparing for Battle

The research facility was a hive of activity as Dr. Emily Carter and Dr. Mark Thompson led their team in preparing for the final showdown with their adversaries. The discovery of the critical vulnerability in the Global Consciousness Network had set off a race against time. Every second counted as they worked to develop and implement the countermeasures needed to protect the GCN.

Emily stood in the main lab, surrounded by monitors displaying real-time data and complex algorithms. Dr. James Lee and his cybersecurity team were hard at work, addressing technical issues and reinforcing the network's defenses.

"James, how are we looking on the countermeasure front?" Emily asked, her eyes scanning the screens.

James looked up, his expression focused but determined. "We've made significant progress. The new encryption protocols are being integrated, and we're setting up additional firewalls. This should help mitigate the vulnerability."

Emily nodded, feeling a surge of hope. "Great work. Keep me updated on any issues."

Meanwhile, in the user support center, Dr. Sarah Mitchell and her team were busy assisting users and gathering feedback. The atmosphere was one of calm efficiency, but the challenges were evident.

"Sarah, how are the users adapting to the new tools and resources?" Emily asked as she entered the room.

Sarah smiled, though her eyes showed signs of fatigue. "The feedback has been mixed. Some users are finding the technology helpful, but others are struggling with the interface and the emotional intensity of the connections. We're working on providing additional training and support."

Emily felt a deep sense of gratitude for her team's dedication. "Thank you, Sarah. Your work is making a real impact. Let's continue to gather feedback and adapt our approach to meet the users' needs."

As the team continued their efforts, they faced significant logistical challenges. In one region, the delivery of essential equipment was delayed due to transportation issues. In another, technical difficulties with the network connectivity posed a barrier to its stability.

Mark, who had been coordinating with external partners and allies, approached Emily with an update. "We've hit a snag with the equipment delivery in the northern region. The roads are in poor condition, and the trucks are having trouble getting through."

Emily sighed, feeling the weight of the obstacles pressing down on her. "Let's explore alternative transportation options. Can we use smaller vehicles or even drones to deliver the equipment?"

Mark nodded, his expression resolute. "I'll coordinate with the logistics team and see what we can do."

In another part of the facility, Emily and Mark met with local partners to address the technical difficulties. They held a series of workshops and training sessions, helping the community members become comfortable with the technology.

An engineer named Carlos spoke up during one of the meetings, his voice filled with concern. "We've been experiencing intermittent connectivity issues. How can we ensure a stable connection?"

Emily felt the weight of his words. "I understand your concerns, Carlos. We're working on optimizing the network to handle the load. We'll deploy additional resources to strengthen the infrastructure and ensure a stable connection."

Mark added, "We're here to listen and learn. This is a partnership, and we want to make sure that the GCN is a positive addition to your community."

As the days turned into nights, the team worked tirelessly to overcome the challenges. They collaborated with local partners, adapted their strategies, and found innovative solutions to the obstacles they faced. Emily felt a deep sense of pride as she watched her colleagues' resilience and determination shine through.

One evening, as the team gathered for a progress update, Ethan presented a breakthrough. "We've identified a way to optimize the network connectivity in the rural areas," he said, his eyes bright with excitement. "By using a combination of satellite and terrestrial networks, we can ensure a stable connection even in the most remote regions."

Emily felt a surge of hope. "That's incredible, Ethan. Let's start working on the implementation immediately."

As the team continued their efforts, they made significant progress in preparing for the final showdown. They addressed technical difficulties, navigated logistical hurdles, and built trust with the communities they served. The journey was far from over, but they were on the right path.

In the quiet moments, Emily reflected on the challenges they had faced and the lessons they had learned. The vision of a connected world, where empathy and understanding transcended barriers, was within reach.

Mark approached her, his eyes filled with a mix of exhaustion and hope. "Emily, we've got a long road ahead, but I believe in what we're doing. The GCN has the potential to change the world, and we're making it happen."

Emily smiled, feeling a renewed sense of purpose. "Thank you, Mark. I couldn't do this without you and the team. Together, we'll overcome these challenges and realize the full potential of the Networked Mind."

In the quiet of the research facility, surrounded by the tools of their groundbreaking work, Emily felt a deep sense of resolve. The journey was far from over, but with the support of her team and the commitment to ethical development, she was ready to lead the way. Together, they would make the vision of the Networked Mind a reality.

The Attack

The research facility was a fortress of activity as Dr. Emily Carter, Dr. Mark Thompson, and their team braced for the impending attack on the Global Consciousness Network. The adversaries had been planning this for months, and now the moment had arrived. The air was thick with tension and determination as the team prepared to defend the GCN.

Emily stood in the cybersecurity lab, surrounded by monitors displaying real-time data and flashing alerts. The hum of computers and the rapid clicking of keyboards filled the room. Dr. James Lee and his cybersecurity team were at their stations, ready to counter any threats.

"Emily, the adversaries are making their move," James reported, his voice steady but urgent. "They're targeting the vulnerability we identified. We need to act fast."

Emily nodded, her mind racing. "Deploy all countermeasures. We can't let them breach the network."

Mark, standing beside her, was coordinating with the rest of the team. "Ethan, we need your insights. How are they managing to sustain such a coordinated attack?"

Ethan, the former hacker who had become an invaluable ally, was at his station, his fingers flying over the keyboard. "They're using a distributed network of bots to amplify their attack. We need to isolate and neutralize the command nodes controlling the bots."

Emily felt a surge of determination. "James, can you pinpoint the command nodes?"

"We're working on it," James replied, his eyes fixed on the screen. "But it's like playing whack-a-mole. Every time we shut one down, another pops up."

The intensity of the attack strained the team's resources and morale. Emily could see the exhaustion in their faces, but she also saw their unwavering resolve. They had come too far to let the adversaries win now.

"Emily, we've identified a pattern," Ethan said, his voice urgent. "They're using a specific sequence to coordinate the bots. If we can disrupt that sequence, we can break their control."

Emily's heart raced. "Do it, Ethan. Disrupt the sequence and shut them down."

Ethan's fingers flew over the keyboard as he executed the countermeasure. The room was filled with a tense silence as they watched the monitors, waiting to see if it would work.

Suddenly, the alerts began to subside. The relentless barrage of attacks slowed, then stopped altogether. The team let out a collective sigh of relief.

"We did it," James said, his voice filled with a mix of exhaustion and triumph. "We've neutralized their attack."

Emily felt a wave of relief wash over her. "Great work, everyone. But we can't let our guard down. They might try again."

As the team continued to monitor the network, Emily and Mark took a moment to reflect on the intensity of the confrontation. They had faced a formidable adversary, but their resilience and teamwork had carried them through.

"Ethan, your insights were invaluable," Mark said, placing a hand on Ethan's shoulder. "We couldn't have done this without you."

Ethan nodded, his expression a mix of relief and determination. "I'm just glad I could help. We need to stay vigilant. They won't give up easily."

Emily felt a deep sense of gratitude for her team's dedication. "Thank you, Ethan. And thank you, everyone. We've faced incredible challenges, but we've proven that we can overcome them together."

As the immediate threat subsided, the team took a moment to regroup and assess the situation. They had successfully defended against the hacker attack, but they knew that the journey was far from over.

In the quiet of the cybersecurity lab, surrounded by the tools of their groundbreaking work, Emily felt a renewed sense of resolve. The journey was far from over, but with the support of her team and the commitment to ethical development, she was ready to lead the way. Together, they would secure the future of the Networked Mind and ensure that it remained a force for good.

The Turning Point

The research facility was a fortress of determination as Dr. Emily Carter, Dr. Mark Thompson, and their team regrouped in the cybersecurity lab. The recent attack on the Global Consciousness Network had been intense, but they had managed to fend it off. Now, they needed to turn the tide and secure the GCN once and for all.

Emily stood at the center of the lab, surrounded by monitors displaying real-time data and flashing alerts. The air was thick with tension and urgency. Dr. James Lee and his cybersecurity team were at their stations, analyzing the adversaries' tactics and looking for any weaknesses.

"Emily, we've identified a critical weakness in their strategy," James reported, his voice steady but urgent. "They're relying heavily on a central command node to coordinate their attacks. If we can take it down, we can disrupt their entire operation."

Emily felt a surge of hope. "That's our chance. We need to exploit that weakness and launch a counterattack."

Mark, standing beside her, was coordinating with the rest of the team. "Ethan, can you pinpoint the location of the command node?"

Ethan, the former hacker who had become an invaluable ally, was at his station, his fingers flying over the keyboard. "I'm on it. Give me a few minutes."

The room was filled with a tense silence as they waited for Ethan to work his magic. Emily could see the exhaustion in their faces, but she also saw their unwavering resolve. They had come too far to let the adversaries win now.

"Got it," Ethan said, his voice filled with excitement. "I've pinpointed the location of the command node. It's heavily guarded, but we can take it down with a coordinated attack."

Emily's heart raced. "James, coordinate with Ethan and prepare the countermeasures. We need to move fast."

James nodded, his expression resolute. "We're on it. Let's take them down."

As the team prepared for the counterattack, Emily and Mark provided leadership and support, ensuring that everyone stayed focused and united. The intensity of the situation was palpable, but they knew that this was their chance to turn the tide.

"Ethan, are you ready?" Emily asked, her voice steady but filled with determination.

Ethan nodded, his eyes fixed on the screen. "Ready."

"James, initiate the countermeasures," Emily commanded.

James's fingers flew over the keyboard as he executed the countermeasures. The room was filled with the hum of computers and the rapid clicking of keyboards as the team worked together to launch the counterattack.

Suddenly, the monitors displayed a series of alerts as the countermeasures took effect. The adversaries' attacks began to falter, their coordination disrupted by the loss of the command node. The team let out a collective sigh of relief as they watched the tide of the battle turn in their favor.

"We did it," James said, his voice filled with a mix of exhaustion and triumph. "We've disrupted their operation."

Emily felt a wave of relief wash over her. "Great work, everyone. But we can't let our guard down. We need to ensure that the GCN remains secure."

As the team continued to monitor the network, Emily and Mark took a moment to reflect on the intensity of the confrontation. They had faced a formidable adversary, but their resilience and teamwork had carried them through.

"Ethan, your insights were invaluable," Mark said, placing a hand on Ethan's shoulder. "We couldn't have done this without you."

Ethan nodded, his expression a mix of relief and determination. "I'm just glad I could help. We need to stay vigilant. They won't give up easily."

Emily felt a deep sense of gratitude for her team's dedication. "Thank you, Ethan. And thank you, everyone. We've faced incredible challenges, but we've proven that we can overcome them together."

As the immediate threat subsided, the team took a moment to regroup and assess the situation. They had successfully defended against the hacker attack, but they knew that the journey was far from over.

In the quiet of the cybersecurity lab, surrounded by the tools of their groundbreaking work, Emily felt a renewed sense of resolve. The journey was far from over, but with the support of her team and the commitment to ethical development, she was ready to lead the way. Together, they would secure the future of the Networked Mind and ensure that it remained a force for good.

Aftermath and Reflection

The research facility was unusually quiet, the hum of the equipment a comforting backdrop as Dr. Emily Carter and Dr. Mark Thompson gathered their team in a small, quiet meeting room. The recent confrontation with the adversaries had been intense, but they had successfully defended the Global Consciousness Network. Now, it was time to reflect on their journey and the challenges they had overcome.

Emily stood at the head of the table, her eyes scanning the faces of her dedicated team. She could see the exhaustion etched into their expressions, but she also saw the spark of determination that had carried them through the crisis.

"Thank you all for being here," Emily began, her voice steady but filled with emotion. "We've faced incredible challenges over the past few weeks, but we've also made significant progress. I wanted to take a moment to acknowledge your hard work and dedication. Your efforts have made a real difference, and I couldn't be prouder to work alongside you."

Dr. James Lee, head of the cybersecurity team, leaned forward. "We've enhanced the security of the GCN and implemented a multi-layered system that adapts to new threats in real-time. The recent attack was a testament to our resilience and our ability to protect the network."

Dr. Sarah Mitchell, the neuroscientist, added, "We've also expanded our mental health resources and support groups, providing users with the tools they need to manage their emotional responses. The feedback from users has been overwhelmingly positive."

Ethan, the former hacker who had joined their efforts, spoke up. "We've made great strides in securing the GCN, but we need to stay vigilant. The hacker group won't give up easily, and we need to be prepared for future challenges."

Emily nodded, her mind racing with the implications of their work. "You're right, Ethan. We need to stay focused and continue to improve the GCN. But I also want to acknowledge the personal sacrifices each of you has made. Your dedication and resilience have been truly inspiring."

Mark, who had been coordinating with external experts, spoke up. "We've also built strong partnerships with leading cybersecurity firms and mental health organizations. Their expertise has been invaluable, and we need to continue to collaborate with them to ensure the GCN remains a force for good."

The room fell silent as the team absorbed the gravity of their journey. Despite their victory, doubts and fears lingered. Emily could see the uncertainty in their eyes, and she knew she needed to inspire them to continue their work.

"Everyone, I know this has been a difficult journey," Emily said, her voice filled with conviction. "But we've proven that we can overcome incredible challenges. The GCN has the potential to change the world, and we are the ones who will make that happen. We need to believe in our vision and stay committed to our mission."

Dr. Karen Foster, the psychologist, nodded in agreement. "We've learned valuable lessons along the way. We've seen the importance of ethical development and the need to prioritize the well-being of our users. These principles will guide us as we move forward."

Emily felt a deep sense of pride as she looked around the room. "Thank you, Karen. And thank you, everyone. Your hard work and dedication have brought us to this point. Let's continue to work together and make the GCN a tool for empathy, understanding, and connection."

As the meeting drew to a close, the team members exchanged words of encouragement and support. They knew the road ahead would be challenging, but they were ready to face whatever obstacles lay in their path.

In the quiet of the meeting room, surrounded by the tools of their groundbreaking work, Emily felt a renewed sense of resolve. The journey was far from over, but with the support of her team and the commitment to ethical development, she was ready to lead the way. Together, they would secure the future of the Networked Mind and ensure that it remained a force for good.

Later that evening, Emily sat at her desk, reflecting on the day's events. She knew that the road ahead would be difficult, but she was ready to face whatever challenges lay ahead. With the support of her team and the commitment to ethical development, she was determined to protect the GCN and realize its full potential.

Mark entered the office, his expression serious but hopeful. "You did great today, Emily. We made it clear that we're taking this seriously and that we're committed to finding solutions."

Emily smiled, feeling a renewed sense of purpose. "Thank you, Mark. We have a lot of work to do, but I believe in the vision of the GCN. Together, we'll find a way to overcome these challenges and create a better, more connected world."

In the quiet of her office, surrounded by the tools of their groundbreaking work, Emily felt a deep sense of resolve. The journey was far from over, but with the support of her team and the commitment to ethical development, she was ready to lead the way. Together, they would make the vision of the Networked Mind a reality.

16

CHAPTER 15: LEGACY

Reflecting on Achievements

The research facility was bathed in the soft glow of the setting sun, casting long shadows across the quiet meeting room. Dr. Emily Carter stood at the head of the table, surrounded by her dedicated team and Ethan, the former hacker who had become an invaluable ally. The air was filled with a sense of accomplishment and reflection as they gathered to look back on their journey and the achievements of the Global Consciousness Network.

"Thank you all for being here," Emily began, her voice steady but filled with emotion. "We've faced incredible challenges over the past few years, but we've also made significant progress. Today, I want to take a moment to reflect on our journey and the positive changes we've brought about."

The large screen behind her displayed a series of data points, testimonials, and images from around the world, each one highlighting the impact of the GCN. Emily clicked through the slides, her heart swelling with pride as she saw the faces of people whose lives had been transformed by their work.

Dr. James Lee, head of the cybersecurity team, leaned forward, his expression one of satisfaction. "We've enhanced the security of the GCN and implemented a multi-layered system that adapts to new threats in real-time. The recent attacks were a testament to our resilience and our ability to protect the network."

Dr. Sarah Mitchell, the neuroscientist, added, "We've also expanded our mental health resources and support groups, providing users with the tools they need to manage their emotional responses. The feedback from users has been overwhelmingly positive."

Ethan, who had played a crucial role in securing the GCN, spoke up. "We've made great strides in ensuring the GCN remains a force for good. But we need to stay vigilant. The challenges we've faced have shown us that we can't afford to be complacent."

Emily nodded, her mind racing with the implications of their work. "You're right, Ethan. We need to stay focused and continue to innovate. But I also want to acknowledge the personal sacrifices each of you has made. Your dedication and resilience have been truly inspiring."

Mark, who had been coordinating with external experts and partners, spoke up. "We've built strong partnerships with leading cybersecurity firms and mental health organizations. Their expertise has been invaluable, and we need to continue to collaborate with them to ensure the GCN remains a force for good."

The room fell silent as the team absorbed the gravity of their journey. Despite their achievements, there were lingering concerns about the future. Emily could see the uncertainty in their eyes, and she knew she needed to inspire them to continue their work.

"Everyone, I know this has been a difficult journey," Emily said, her voice filled with conviction. "But we've proven that we can overcome incredible challenges. The GCN has the potential to change the world, and we are the ones who will make that happen. We need to believe in our vision and stay committed to our mission."

Dr. Karen Foster, the psychologist, nodded in agreement. "We've learned valuable lessons along the way. We've seen the importance of ethical development and the need to prioritize the well-being of our users. These principles will guide us as we move forward."

Emily felt a deep sense of pride as she looked around the room. "Thank you, Karen. And thank you, everyone. Your hard work and dedication have brought us to this point. Let's continue to work together and make the GCN a tool for empathy, understanding, and connection."

As the meeting drew to a close, the team members exchanged words of encouragement and support. They knew the road ahead would be challenging, but they were ready to face whatever obstacles lay in their path.

In the quiet of the meeting room, surrounded by the tools of their groundbreaking work, Emily felt a renewed sense of resolve. The journey was far from over, but with the support of her team and the commitment to ethical development, she was ready to lead the way. Together, they would secure the future of the Networked Mind and ensure that it remained a force for good.

Later that evening, Emily sat at her desk, reflecting on the day's events. She knew that the road ahead would be difficult, but she was ready to face whatever challenges lay ahead. With the support of her team and the commitment to ethical development, she was determined to protect the GCN and realize its full potential.

Mark entered the office, his expression serious but hopeful. "You did great today, Emily. We made it clear that we're taking this seriously and that we're committed to finding solutions."

Emily smiled, feeling a renewed sense of purpose. "Thank you, Mark. We have a lot of work to do, but I believe in the vision of the GCN. Together, we'll find a way to overcome these challenges and create a better, more connected world."

In the quiet of her office, surrounded by the tools of their groundbreaking work, Emily felt a deep sense of resolve. The journey was far from over, but with the support of her team and the commitment to ethical development, she was ready to lead the way. Together, they would make the vision of the Networked Mind a reality.

Honoring the Contributors

The research facility was transformed into a place of celebration as Dr. Emily Carter and Dr. Mark Thompson prepared to host an awards ceremony. The large atrium, usually filled with the hum of scientific equipment and the focused energy of researchers, was now adorned with elegant decorations and filled with the buzz of excited conversations. This evening was dedicated to honoring the contributors who had played a crucial role in the development and success of the Global Consciousness Network.

Emily stood at the entrance, greeting guests as they arrived. She felt a mix of pride and gratitude as she saw the familiar faces of her team, external partners, and allies. Each person had contributed to the GCN in their own unique way, and tonight was a chance to celebrate their collective effort.

"Emily, this is wonderful," Mark said, joining her at the entrance. "It's important to take a moment to recognize everyone's hard work and dedication."

Emily nodded, her heart swelling with pride. "Absolutely. We've come so far, and it's all thanks to the incredible people who believed in our vision."

As the guests mingled and found their seats, Emily and Mark took their places on the stage. The room fell silent as Emily stepped up to the podium, her eyes scanning the crowd.

"Good evening, everyone," she began, her voice steady but filled with emotion. "Thank you all for being here tonight. We are here to celebrate the incredible achievements of the Global Consciousness Network and to honor the contributors who made it all possible."

The large screen behind her displayed a series of images and videos, each one highlighting the impact of the GCN. Emily clicked through the slides, her heart swelling with pride as she saw the faces of people whose lives had been transformed by their work.

"Over the past few years, we have faced incredible challenges," Emily continued. "But we have also made significant progress. The GCN has brought people together, fostered empathy and understanding, and provided support to those in need. None of this would have been possible without the hard work and dedication of each and every one of you."

Mark stepped forward to join her. "Tonight, we want to recognize the contributions of our team, our partners, and our allies. Your efforts have made a real difference, and we are incredibly grateful for your support."

As they began to present the awards, the room was filled with applause and cheers. Dr. James Lee was recognized for his outstanding work in cybersecurity, ensuring the safety and integrity of the GCN. Dr. Sarah Mitchell received an award for her contributions to mental health support, providing users with the tools they needed to manage their emotional responses.

Ethan, the former hacker who had become an invaluable ally, was also honored. "Ethan, your insights and expertise have been crucial to our success," Emily said, her voice filled with gratitude. "Thank you for your dedication and for believing in our vision."

Ethan stepped up to the stage, his expression a mix of pride and humility. "Thank you, Emily. It's been an incredible journey, and I'm proud to be a part of it."

As the ceremony continued, Emily felt a deep sense of fulfillment. Each award presented was a testament to the collective effort and unwavering dedication of their team. But she also knew that the journey had not been without its sacrifices.

After the ceremony, Emily mingled with the guests, listening to their stories and reflecting on the challenges they had faced. She could see the mixed emotions in their eyes—pride in their achievements, but also the weight of the personal sacrifices they had made.

Dr. Karen Foster, the psychologist, approached her, her expression thoughtful. "Emily, tonight has been wonderful. But I can't help but think about the toll this journey has taken on all of us."

Emily nodded, her heart heavy with understanding. "I know, Karen. We've all made sacrifices, and it's important to acknowledge that. But I also believe that our work has made a real difference. We've created something that has the potential to change the world."

Karen smiled, her eyes filled with warmth. "You're right, Emily. And tonight has reminded me of why we do what we do. Thank you for bringing us all together."

As the evening drew to a close, Emily and Mark stood at the entrance, thanking the guests as they left. The room was filled with a sense of camaraderie and shared purpose, a reminder of the incredible journey they had been on.

"Emily, tonight was a success," Mark said, his voice filled with satisfaction. "We've recognized the hard work and dedication of our team, and we've inspired them to continue their efforts."

Emily smiled, feeling a renewed sense of purpose. "Thank you, Mark. We have a lot of work to do, but I believe in the vision of the GCN. Together, we'll find a way to overcome these challenges and create a better, more connected world."

In the quiet of the research facility, surrounded by the tools of their groundbreaking work, Emily felt a deep sense of resolve. The journey was far from over, but with the support of her team and the commitment to ethical development, she was ready to lead the way. Together, they would make the vision of the Networked Mind a reality.

Passing the Torch

The research facility was quiet, the hum of the equipment a familiar backdrop as Dr. Emily Carter and Dr. Mark Thompson prepared for an important meeting. Today, they would be passing the torch to a new generation of researchers who would carry on the work of the Global Consciousness Network. The thought filled Emily with a mix of pride and nostalgia. She had dedicated so much of her life to the GCN, and now it was time to ensure its legacy continued.

Emily stood in her office, reviewing her notes one last time. The large window behind her offered a view of the facility's grounds, bathed in the soft light of the morning sun. She took a deep breath, feeling a sense of calm and determination.

Mark entered the office, his expression serious but supportive. "Emily, they're ready. Are you?"

Emily nodded, her resolve firm. "Let's do this."

They walked together to the conference room, where a group of young researchers awaited them. The room was filled with a sense of anticipation and excitement. These bright minds represented the future of the GCN, and Emily was eager to share her experiences and offer guidance.

"Good morning, everyone," Emily began, her voice steady but warm. "Thank you all for being here. Today is an important day for the Global Consciousness Network. We are passing the torch to you, the next generation of researchers who will carry on our work and ensure the GCN's legacy continues."

The young researchers listened intently, their eyes filled with curiosity and determination. Emily could see the potential in each of them, and it filled her with hope.

Mark stepped forward to join her. "We've faced incredible challenges over the past few years, but we've also made significant progress. The GCN has brought people together, fostered empathy and understanding, and provided support to those in need. None of this would have been possible without the hard work and dedication of our team."

Emily continued, "We want to share our experiences with you, offer guidance, and emphasize the importance of ethical development. The GCN is a powerful tool, and with great power comes great responsibility. It's up to you to ensure that it remains a force for good."

One of the young researchers, a woman named Maya, raised her hand. "Dr. Carter, what advice do you have for us as we take on this responsibility?"

Emily smiled, appreciating the thoughtful question. "My advice is to stay true to your values and always prioritize the well-being of the users. The GCN was created to foster empathy and understanding, and it's important to keep that vision at the forefront of your work. Collaborate with others, listen to feedback, and be open to new ideas. And most importantly, never lose sight of the ethical implications of your work."

Another researcher, a man named Alex, spoke up. "What were some of the biggest challenges you faced, and how did you overcome them?"

Mark responded, "One of the biggest challenges was ensuring the security and privacy of the GCN. We faced numerous attacks and had to constantly adapt our strategies to protect the network. It required a lot of teamwork, resilience, and innovation. We also had to navigate the ethical implications of our work and ensure that we were always acting in the best interests of the users."

Emily added, "Another challenge was building trust with the public and addressing their concerns. We had to be transparent and accountable, and we worked hard to engage in dialogue and find common ground. It wasn't always easy, but it was essential to our success."

The young researchers nodded, absorbing the wisdom and insights shared by Emily and Mark. They asked more questions, eager to learn from the experiences of their predecessors.

As the meeting continued, Emily felt a deep sense of fulfillment. She could see the passion and dedication in the eyes of the young researchers, and it reassured her that the GCN was in good hands.

"Thank you for your questions and for your commitment to the GCN," Emily said, her voice filled with emotion. "We believe in you, and we are confident that you will carry on our work with integrity and dedication. The future of the GCN is bright, and we are excited to see what you will achieve."

As the meeting drew to a close, the young researchers expressed their gratitude and excitement for the journey ahead. Emily and Mark felt a renewed sense of purpose, knowing that they had inspired the next generation to continue their mission.

In the quiet of the conference room, surrounded by the tools of their groundbreaking work, Emily felt a deep sense of resolve. The journey was far from over, but with the support of the new generation and the commitment to ethical development, she was ready to lead the way. Together, they would make the vision of the Networked Mind a reality.

A Global Impact

The research facility was alive with a sense of accomplishment as Dr. Emily Carter and Dr. Mark Thompson gathered their team to observe the global impact of the Global Consciousness Network. The large conference room was filled with the hum of excitement and anticipation. Today, they would see firsthand how their work had brought people together and fostered empathy and understanding across the world.

Emily stood at the front of the room, her heart swelling with pride as she looked at the faces of her dedicated team. The large screen behind her displayed a world map, dotted with locations where the GCN had made a significant impact. Each dot represented a community, a family, or an individual whose life had been transformed by their work.

"Thank you all for being here," Emily began, her voice steady but filled with emotion. "Today, we are here to celebrate the global impact of the GCN. We have worked tirelessly to create a tool that fosters empathy and understanding, and now we get to see the fruits of our labor."

Dr. James Lee, head of the cybersecurity team, leaned forward, his expression one of satisfaction. "We've received testimonials from users around the world, sharing stories of how the GCN has changed their lives. It's incredible to see the positive impact we've made."

Dr. Sarah Mitchell, the neuroscientist, added, "We've also seen a significant increase in mental health support and resources. The GCN has provided a platform for people to connect and share their experiences, reducing feelings of isolation and fostering a sense of community."

Ethan, the former hacker who had become an invaluable ally, spoke up. "We've made great strides in ensuring the GCN remains a force for good. But we need to stay vigilant and continue to innovate to meet the needs of diverse populations."

Emily nodded, her mind racing with the implications of their work. "You're right, Ethan. We need to stay focused and continue to adapt. But today, let's take a moment to celebrate our achievements and the positive change we've created."

As the team watched the screen, they saw testimonials from users around the world. A teacher in a rural village in India shared how the GCN had connected her students with educators from around the globe, providing them with new opportunities and perspectives. A mental health counselor in Brazil spoke about how the GCN had helped her clients feel less isolated and more understood.

One testimonial, in particular, stood out to Emily. A young woman named Amina from a remote village in Africa shared her story. "The GCN has changed my life," Amina said, her voice filled with emotion. "I used to feel so alone, but now I can connect with people from all over the world. I've made friends, found support, and learned so much. Thank you for creating this incredible tool."

Emily felt a lump form in her throat as she listened to Amina's words. This was why they had worked so hard, why they had faced so many challenges. To make a difference in people's lives, to bring them together and foster understanding.

Mark, standing beside her, placed a hand on her shoulder. "Emily, this is incredible. We've created something truly special."

Emily smiled, feeling a deep sense of fulfillment. "Thank you, Mark. And thank you, everyone. Your hard work and dedication have made this possible. Let's continue to work together and ensure that the GCN remains a force for good."

As the meeting continued, the team discussed the challenges they faced in maintaining the network's integrity while expanding its reach. They knew that they needed to stay vigilant and continue to innovate to meet the needs of diverse populations.

Dr. Karen Foster, the psychologist, voiced her concerns. "We need to ensure that the GCN continues to evolve and adapt. The needs of our users are constantly changing, and we need to be proactive in addressing those needs."

Emily nodded, her resolve strengthening. "You're right, Karen. We need to stay focused and continue to innovate. But today, let's take a moment to celebrate our achievements and the positive change we've created."

As the meeting drew to a close, the team members exchanged words of encouragement and support. They knew the road ahead would be challenging, but they were ready to face whatever obstacles lay in their path.

In the quiet of the conference room, surrounded by the tools of their groundbreaking work, Emily felt a renewed sense of resolve. The journey was far from over, but with the support of her team and the commitment to ethical development, she was ready to lead the way. Together, they would secure the future of the Networked Mind and ensure that it remained a force for good.

Later that evening, Emily sat at her desk, reflecting on the day's events. She knew that the road ahead would be difficult, but she was ready to face whatever challenges lay ahead. With the support of her team and the commitment to ethical development, she was determined to protect the GCN and realize its full potential.

Mark entered the office, his expression serious but hopeful. "You did great today, Emily. We made it clear that we're taking this seriously and that we're committed to finding solutions."

Emily smiled, feeling a renewed sense of purpose. "Thank you, Mark. We have a lot of work to do, but I believe in the vision of the GCN. Together, we'll find a way to overcome these challenges and create a better, more connected world."

In the quiet of her office, surrounded by the tools of their groundbreaking work, Emily felt a deep sense of resolve. The journey was far from

over, but with the support of her team and the commitment to ethical development, she was ready to lead the way. Together, they would make the vision of the Networked Mind a reality.

Looking to the Future

The research facility was abuzz with anticipation as Dr. Emily Carter and Dr. Mark Thompson prepared for the global press conference. The past few years had been a whirlwind of innovation, challenges, and triumphs, and today, they would share their vision for the future of the Global Consciousness Network. The large atrium, usually filled with the hum of scientific equipment and focused researchers, was now transformed into a stage for this momentous occasion.

Emily stood in front of the mirror in her office, adjusting her blazer and taking a deep breath. She felt a mix of exhaustion and determination. This was their moment to show the world that they were committed to ethical development and transparency.

Mark knocked on the door, his expression serious but supportive. "Emily, it's time. Are you ready?"

Emily nodded, her resolve strengthening. "Let's do this."

They walked together to the press conference room, where a sea of reporters and cameras awaited them. The room buzzed with anticipation, the air thick with tension. Emily and Mark took their places at the podium, the bright lights casting harsh shadows on their faces. Beside them stood representatives from their team, external partners, and even some of the resistance members who had become allies.

"Good morning," Emily began, her voice steady but filled with emotion. "Thank you all for being here. Over the past few years, we have worked tirelessly to develop and expand the Global Consciousness Network. Today, we are here to share our vision for the future and outline our plans for continued innovation, ethical development, and global collaboration."

The large screen behind her flickered to life, displaying a series of data points, maps, and testimonials from users around the world. Emily clicked through the slides, highlighting key achievements and milestones.

"We have listened to the concerns of our users and have worked together to address them," Emily continued. "Our goal is to create a framework that protects privacy and autonomy while fostering empathy and understanding. This vision is at the heart of everything we do."

Mark stepped forward to provide more details. "We have implemented new privacy and security measures, established an independent oversight committee, and involved representatives from diverse sectors in our decision-making process. We believe that by working together, we can create a better, more connected world."

A reporter raised her hand, her expression serious. "Dr. Carter, how can you reassure the public that the GCN will continue to evolve ethically and responsibly?"

Emily took a deep breath, her resolve unwavering. "We understand the public's concerns, and we are committed to addressing them. The oversight committee will include representatives from various sectors, including ethics, law, and human rights. Our goal is to ensure that the GCN is used responsibly and for the benefit of all."

Another reporter asked, "What are your plans for further expansion? How do you ensure that the GCN remains a force for good as it continues to grow?"

Mark addressed the question with confidence. "We are committed to continuous improvement and ethical development. We will work closely with the oversight committee and external experts to ensure that the GCN remains a force for good. Our focus is on fostering empathy and understanding, and we will do everything in our power to protect that vision."

The press conference continued, with Emily and Mark addressing a range of questions and sharing their vision for the future. They knew that rebuilding public trust would take time and consistent effort, but they were determined to show their commitment to making the GCN safe and beneficial for everyone.

As the press conference drew to a close, Emily felt a mix of exhaustion and determination. They had faced the public, acknowledged the challenges, and outlined their plan to address them. It was a crucial step forward, but the journey was far from over.

Back in her office, Emily sat down at her desk, her mind racing with the events of the day. She knew that the road ahead would be difficult, but she was ready to face whatever challenges lay ahead. With the support of her team and the commitment to ethical development, she was determined to protect the GCN and realize its full potential.

Mark entered the office, his expression serious but hopeful. "You did great today, Emily. We made it clear that we're taking this seriously and that we're committed to finding solutions."

Emily smiled, feeling a renewed sense of purpose. "Thank you, Mark. We have a lot of work to do, but I believe in the vision of the GCN. Together, we'll find a way to overcome these challenges and create a better, more connected world."

In the quiet of her office, surrounded by the tools of their groundbreaking work, Emily felt a deep sense of resolve. The journey was far from over, but with the support of her team and the commitment to ethical development, she was ready to lead the way. Together, they would make the vision of the Networked Mind a reality.